ISBN 978-1-4400-6770-9
PIBN 10020206

1 MONTH OF
FREE
READING

at

www.ForgottenBooks.com

By purchasing this book you are eligible for one month membership to ForgottenBooks.com, giving you unlimited access to our entire collection of over 700,000 titles via our web site and mobile apps.

To claim your free month visit:

www.forgottenbooks.com/free20206

English
Français
Deutsche
Italiano
Español
Português

www.forgottenbooks.com

Mythology Photography **Fiction**
Fishing Christianity **Art** Cooking
Essays Buddhism Freemasonry
Medicine **Biology** Music **Ancient
Egypt** Evolution Carpentry Physics
Dance Geology **Mathematics** Fitness
Shakespeare **Folklore** Yoga Marketing
Confidence Immortality Biographies
Poetry **Psychology** Witchcraft
Electronics Chemistry History **Law**
Accounting **Philosophy** Anthropology
Alchemy Drama Quantum Mechanics
Atheism Sexual Health **Ancient History**
Entrepreneurship Languages Sport
Paleontology Needlework Islam
Metaphysics Investment Archaeology
Parenting Statistics Criminology
Motivational

OUR STORY

OF

ATLANTIS.

Written down for the

HERMETIC BROTHERHOOD

By W. P. PHELON, M. D.

Author of "THREE SEVENS"; "HEALING, CAUSES AND
EFFECT"; "LOVE, SEX, IMMORTALITY." Etc.

SAN FRANCISCO, CALIF.
HERMETIC BOOK CONCERN.
1903.

BLACK OAT PRESS, 402 M'ALLSTER ST., S. F.

GENERAL HEADQUARTERS

976

In tl

FOREWORD.

It is not necessary for an author in these later days, always to be able to say, he writes of his own knowledge. This has become a recognized fact. He may write from another's experience, in whose honesty and reliability, he has as much, and sometimes more confidence, than in his own personal sense. This is the case with this little book, treating of a subject of interest to the whole world, to-day. For six years I have had the MSS. almost ready for the printer. Now, with the encouragement and helping hand of my Dear Comrades of the Hermetic Brotherhood, I am bid to let it go forth. May it be a help to the ONCE ATLANTIAN BORN, wherever they may be.

W. P. PHELON, M. D.

CONTENTS

of Instruction. The wonderful play of visible form and color, never equaled elsewhere in the whole world, before or since. Supremely dominant now, in the affairs of the world.

CHAPTER XVI.

The Cellars of the Great Elemental Mint and Treasury, under the Temple. Their occupants, uses and the influences upon the State and world, then and nów. Date of the opening of these Treasuries to the inspection of the Temple Inspector.

CHAPTER XVII.

The Treasury of the Temple; its contents and uses.

CHAPTER XVIII.

Concerning Convocations. The kinds and methods of calling and their uses and influence even upon the world of to-day.

CHAPTER XIX.

The Messiah that must come is a nation and not an individual. It was the stone cut out of the mountain without hands. For this work and wait.

CHAPTER XX.

We, as Atlantians, did not break the law; but we made a mistake. For our ignorance, we suffered. The iustrument cannot be superior to the Maker and User.

CHAPTER XXI.

Corroborating evidence from the news of the present day, as it comes to the ears of the "Watchers on the Walls,"—Atlantis, Egypt, India.

OUR STORY OF ATLANTIS.

CHAPTER I.

THE LOST ATLANTIS.

FAIR Atlantis, peerless country!
Lulled within the Ocean's arms,
Lying beautiful and shining
Far beneath the storm's alarms;
Never has a plague come near thee;
In thy halls were love and ease;
Now, above thee lost Atlantis!
Roll the ever restless seas.

In those histories, half tradition,
With their mythical thread of gold,
We shall find the name and story

Of thy cities, fair and old;
Dreaming bard has told in fancy
Wandering minstrel sung of thee,
Now, above thee, lost Atlantis,
Rolls the ever restless sea.

Every heart has such a country;
Some Atlantis loved, and lost—
Where upon the gleaming sand bars
Once life's fitful ocean tost;
Mighty cities rose in splendor,
Love was monarch of that clime
Now, above that lost Atlantis
Rolls the restless sea of Time.

Happy he, who looking backward
From a life of larger scope
Deems a youthful idle fancy
His lost continent of Hope;
Or by light of love and gladness,
Find the present home sublime
Glad that over his Atlantis
Rolls the restless sea of Time.

Why is this book written? is the most pertinent

question asked an author at the outset of composition. It is echoed and re-echoed by critic and reader upon its publication. It certainly appears to be a fair question whenever, the subjects seem so much out of the route of ordinary information, as the present volume.

The scattered records of the Past, within the historical period, would apparently yield scarcely enough material to make a short magazine article of any interest, to say nothing of swelling in size, to the dignity of a book.

It is now conceded, however, by our wisest scientists, that every configuration and corresponding circumstance points to the possibility of the existence of an island continent in the neighborhood, if not directly over the great West Indian Archipelago, just as the whole configuration of the North American Continent tells the story of the inland sea that broke through its barriers at the Thousand Islands in the St. Lawrence river, and hurling itself over Niagara Falls, left the habitable valley of the Mississippi, as a legacy to man for future settlement.

The sacred writings of all nations concur in the same declaration and statement of disaster to some portion of the earth, most generally including all. In a late issue of Mind, appears an article headed: "A Monument to Atlantis," which says: "A notable discovery of more than ordinary interest for historians, especially those who have a leaning toward antiquities, has lately been made by the well-known archaeologist, Augustus Le Plongeon. This discovery should particularly attract the attention of Americans, since it enables them to lay claim to one of the most important monuments of ancient times. The edifice in question is the Pyramid of Xochicalo, standing 5,396 feet above the level of the sea, and situated to the south-southwest of Cuernavaca, 60 miles from the City of Mexico. For more than a century the pyramid has been occasionally visited by distinguished travelers, including the learned Hum-

boldt; but none succeeded in discovering the purpose for which the monument had been erected,
nor in deciphering the mysterious inscriptions on
its sides.

As far back as 1886, Dr. *Le* Plongeon pub-
lished his alphabetic key to the Maya hieroglyphs,
comparing this with the ancient Egyptian hieratic
alphabet. He has now found that the signs on
the Pyramid of Xochicalo are both Maya and
Egyptian; and a careful study of these decorative
inscriptions has made it plain to him that the
pyramid was a monumental structure erected to
commemorate the submergence and destruction of
the great Land of Mu (Plato's Atlantis), together with its population of 64,000,000 of human beings, about 11,500 years ago.

Dr. *Le* Plongeon, in his remarkable work,
"Queen Moo and the Egyptian Sphinx," gives
four Maya accounts of the same cataclysm. This,
then, is the fifth, and, in his own opinion, the
most important of all the known records in Maya

language of the appalling event that gave rise to the story of a universal Deluge that is found in the sacred books of the Jews, the Christians and the Mohammedans.

These records, on stone, on sun-dried bricks, on papyrus, all tell the same story. The little we know of the Aztecs is also confirmatory of the same fact. Whence came the people of South America, with their advanced civilization and traditions of the Past? What mighty people built the great cities and temples of the now forest-covered cities of Yucatain and Central America, with their carved glyphs, and correspondencies to the hieroglyphs of the Valley of the Nile and the East Indian entablatures; and moreover, on almost precisely similar styles of architecture to those of Egypt and India. Is it reasonable to suppose there was no common bond of fellowship between all these? The Ancient Egyptian ideas have dominated the world down to the present day. Instead of a mummy-case, we use a coffin for our dead. The idea is the same—the departed ghost was to be saved the trouble of making a new body, perhaps at short notice, at the great day of the resurrection.

The trinity in unity of God, now universally received, was an Egyptian idea, and the same is wrought into the stone tablets which *La Plongeon* and his amiable wife have unearthed in the forests of the Maias and Quiches.

If the nation, of which these are but the feeble remnants, had not disappeared by some cataclysmal climax we must certainly have had some later, historical data. As the mind of the present generation is more largely than ever, desirous of Truth, the idea of Astral presentation and perception may not be without its weight, especially as the books of Wisdom of the Past declare, that automatic books of record are kept of all deeds and manifestation, upon the earth.

It may be asked, why, those who have entered into the rest of the Unseen should be at all con-

cerned in the unfoldment and development of the
race, who are ever toiling over the rocky paths of
the planet? If the doctrine of re-incarnation is
true, then would it not be to the interest of the
coming Egos, for all the race of men to be advanced just as far as possible, so that the re-incarnated from time to time, might receive the
highest advantage attainable, from their touch
with the earth, at any particular time. Those
who are coming back into the present civilization,
if they were of the advanced and cultured classes
of Atlantis and the most ancient Egypt, would
find more advantages of acquirement, through
our leisure and experience, than when hurled into
life amid the horrors and darkness of the Stone
Age.

From time to time, the material and data obtained as hereinafter described, from which this
book is made, has been pressed upon my attention,
as something that would be of use, and interest
to all who are seeking to KNOW. I do not

doubt the authenticity of my information, nor
the statements given as facts, by those who were
so kind and courteous as to make the writer their
mouthpiece in this re-collection of the ancient
memories.

I do not doubt, that to many readers, will
come fleeting glimpses of these scenes, as if they
had been part of them. It is a conceded fact,
there have never been, since the fall of Atlantis,
so many re-incarnated Atlantians upon the earth
at the same time, as now. This accounts for the
almost universal demand out of the Astral records
for the forgotten knowledge of the occult, which
they there recorded. This also explains the readi-
ness of the public mind to receive knowledge of
the doctrines of Mental Healing, Spiritualism,
Theosophy, and occultism in all its branches.

Ignatius Donnelly finds a supporter of his
Atlantis theory in Sir Daniel Wilson, president
of the University of Toronto, who declares after
a great deal of search, that the lost Atlantis was

not a myth, but that it was really a part of the continent of America. He accounts for its disappearance from view in a different way, but that is merely incidental.

Donnelly's theory was that the land was submerged by some great volcanic upheaval, and that from those who escaped to the continents of Europe and Asia came the tradition of the deluge. Sir Daniel rejects this explanation as being disproved by the fact that there are no traces of such volcanic action either on the continent or in the ocean bed. He believes that the ancient Egyptians, the most progressive and adventurous people of ancient times, discovered the continent, but that in the decline both of their learning and power, it became lost to view and existed at the time our knowledge of Egypt begins merely as a shadowy tradition.

It is his opinion that traces of the Egyptians of those days are to be sought in the ruined cities of Central America, whose origin has never been determined nor even been made the basis of any reasonable theory. Such a discovery would furnish a substantial basis for the legend of the lost Atlantis and the theory invests those wonderful ruins with a new interest for the antiquarians.

The St. Louis Republic said: "Atlantis was a continent supposed to have existed at a very early period in the Atlantic Ocean, over against the Pillars of Hercules," but which was subsequently sunk in a cataclysm of which history gives no record. Plato is the first who gives an account of it, and he is said to have obtained his information from some Egyptian priests with whom he had come in contact. Plato's account says: "Atlantis was a continent larger than Asia and Africa put together, and that at its western extremity were islands which afforded easy passage to a large continent lying still beyond— this last mentioned continent being now supposed to be South America." Nine thousand years before the time of Plato, according to the tradition, Atlantis was a powerful, thickly settled-country which extended its way over Africa and the major portion of what is now Europe, "even to as far as the Tyrrhenian Sea." Further progress of the invasion of the Atlantides was checked by the combined efforts of the Athenians and other Greeks. Shortly after the invaders were driven from the continents of Europe and Africa a great earthquake shook Atlantis from center to circumference. First, the outlying islands sank; then great areas of the mainland. Waves ran mountain high across hundreds of square miles of what had the day before been fertile fields. Great temples were racked and riven; and the affrighted populace climbed upon the ruins to escape the encroaching waters. On the second day, after a night of terrors which no pen could possibly describe, the earthquake shocks were of greatly increased violence, ending only after the entire continent had been engulfed. There is no page in history or tradition that records a more frightful catastrophe, and nothing would be of more absorbing interest than a work entirely devoted to giving an account of what is known concerning it.

To the objector who urges that the explorers of the world have never discovered any traces of the great city and continent, whose story I have endeavored to give in the following pages; permit me to give a few straws floating on our sea of current literature, which show that the history of past ages may yet be read in the Central part of our continent:

"The recent report that a citizen of the United States has discovered among the mountains of the Mexican State of Sinaloa a long-forgotten city tallies with a curious local tradition of the region. Adjoining the State of Sinaloa on the south is the State of Jallisco, and of this State, Guadalajara is the capital. Living in the mountains of Jallisco, part of the great Sierra Madre or

"Mother Range" that extends through Sinaloa and thence northward, are the unconquered Yaquis, a brown-haired people with light eyes and almost fair complexions. Guadalajara is the only civilized town that these Yaquis visit, and it has long been believed there that the Yaquis fastnesses of the Sierra Madre range conceal not only rich mines of silver, but as well the lost city of the Aztec race. No one has hitherto pierced the mountain wilderness, because the naked Yaquis have an effective system of passive resistance that has hitherto successfully closed the sole line of approach. The only human beings other than the Yaquis themselves admitted to the mountains of Jallisco are a few renegade Apaches, murderous wretches, vastly more dangerous to would-be explorers than the peaceful but persistent Yaquis."

There is no question in the minds of those who have given attention to the subject, that the Aztecs are the lineal descendants of the mighty nation who sought to know beyond the law governing the created. Of the unknown city above mentioned, we add another description from a different source:

"During the frequent visits I have made to Mexico," said a mining engineer of Philadelphia to an Inquirer reporter, "I have come in contact with many of the Indians resident there and have heard some very singular stories. One which all the Indians unite in telling, is that far in the interior exists an enormous city, never yet visited by white men. It is described as peopled by a race similar to the ancient Aztecs, who are sun worshipers and offer human sacrifices to their deity.

"The race is said to be in a high state of civilization, and the Indians say that the city is full of huge structures which are miracles of quaint but beautiful architecture, and are situated on broad paved streets, far surpassing those of the City of Mexico.

"One Indian, I recollect, assured me that he had seen the city and its inhabitants with his own eyes, but had been afraid of being captured and had fled. Of course, I did not believe him, but, all the same, it is not a little strange that the accounts of the Mexican Indians, relative to the mysterious and magnificent, interior city agree perfectly."

These are but of many of the allusions and traditions pointing to the fact, that somewhere in the Southwest, there is a people who undoubtedly hold a complete historical record of the chain of events from Atlantis in its prime, down to the present day. While there is perhaps but a single city inhabited and secluded from the outside world of to-day as keepers of the Ancient Wisdom, we yet find ruins of such magnitude as to impress us more strongly with the idea that the people who builded the original structures, could not have wholly disappeared from this Continent. The following from San Diego, Cal., we offer in proof, calling attention to the fact that the dragon is a favorite design in the East Indian sculptures:

"The ruins of a prehistoric city have just been discovered by a party of prospectors from Yuma when on the Colorado desert in search of the Pegleg mine. The wind had laid bare the walls and the remains of the stone buildings a distance of 420 feet in length by 260 feet in width. Gigantic pillars, quaintly carved to represent dragons' heads and rattlesnakes, still stood in the sands of the desert, supporting on their tops huge slabs of granite weighing many tons. The frieze ornamentation resembled Egyptian sculptures and exhibited a greater degree of skill than is possessed by the Indian artisans of the present day. Fragments of pottery were found underneath the debris, and together with the crumbled piece of frieze were brought by one of the party, to this city. One of his associates came to San Diego and the others returned to Yuma, nearly two weeks ago. But the story of their discovery was carefully guarded, in the hope that in some way they might profit by it.

"The discoverers, in company with four others, afterwards went to the desert to explore the ruins. They were driven back by a sand storm, reaching this city to-day, but will make a careful examination of the ruins in the season when the conditions are favorable for extensive explorations. From the relics exhibited it is evident that an important archeaeological discovery has been made."

In connection with the above, there is a peculiarity to be noticed in the occurrence of the sand storm. It has always been so. A storm or some sudden natural event has warded off all efforts to reach these wonderful remains of the prehistoric, or even the existing cities. When men shall be ready to seek them, desiring knowledge and not treasure, there is no doubt the keys for the unlocking of the mysteries of the Past,

will be given into worthy hands and what we
have herein written will receive ample corroboration. We add still another account of wonderful discovery in proof of the immense population of the old Atlantian kingdom in its prime.
This time, it is from the City of Mexico, the
center of the modern Atlantian or Aztec civilization:

"What appears to be the verification of an old
Aztec fable of a buried race of cave-dwellers and
a hidden city in southwestern Mexico is a matter
in which the local scientists are interested at
present. L. P. Leroyal, a French engineer, who
has lived long in this republic, has just arrived
form the wilds of the Southwest and reported
that he has discovered in the State of Guerrero
a huge natural cave, which he believes to be the
greatest in Mexico, if not in the world. He says
it is much larger than the famous cavern of Caca-
huamilpa, situated some distance south of Guer-
navaca, which has hitherto been supposed to be

the largest natural cave in existence in Mexico. Mr. Leroyal, after penetrating a considerable distance into the cave, determined to make a thorough investigation of it, and accordingly a few days ago furnished himself with food sufficient for a day, provided himself with lanterns, etc., and set out upon his task all alone. As he went along he made a thorough plan of the cave, but did not anticipate that his task would be so arduous as it proved. At the first, the bottom of the cave was a gradual slope downward, then changed upward and afterward alternated for the most part between descents and ascents. Here and there, however, a level bottom of great width was met. The height of the cave varied, as might naturally be expected; in some places it was several hundred feet high. For some distance from the entrance no trace of human beings was found. Occasionally magnificent stalactites and stalagmites, the finest Mr. Leroyal had ever seen, were met with.

"After proceeding for some hours he came upon what had evidently been an ancient cemetery, as there were at least 400 petrified bodies, together with ancient idols, etc. There was also a fountain of beautiful clear spring water which was found to be excellent. Some of the tools, as well as two or three skulls, Mr. Leroyal brought away with him, and they are now in this city. The appearance of this charnel house thus lighted up for the first time for hundreds of years was grewsome in the extreme and well calculated to shake the nerves of the explorer. Mr. Leroyal continued his explorations while hour after hour passed. It was not until after he had traveled a distance of at least twenty-one and one-half leagues that he thought it time to call a halt and proceed on his return journey. So far as he could see the distance still to be traversed might be very considerable, with the chances for the cave opening out, as the floor seemed to be well trodden by human feet. He retraced his steps as speedily as possible, and after being underground for upward of twenty-four hours, found himself once more at the entrance of the cave. Mr. Leroyal promised to make further explorations before long. It is expected that a party fully equipped for the exploration of this wonderful cavern of the dead, will soon be fitted out under the guidance of the discoverer, and the outcome of the investigations will be awaited with interest. The natives of the locality, as, in fact, the Indian population in general, in Mexico, believe that at some place near the southwestern coast of Mexico there exists a great white city with countless treasure which has never been seen by white men, and the approach to which is so intricate and cleverly concealed that a stranger has never entered its solitary precincts."

With all the increasing mass of information on the subject, it seems there should be some effort at collection under guidance, of what is known about Atlantis the Mighty. To make a beginning and thus call attention in this direction is 'my answer to the question: "Why this book is written."

ATLANTIAN MEMORIES.

Out of the dim Past, old memories come to me;
From where the light in all its glory seemed to be,
As the people worshiped 'near the Sun's resplendent
     rays
And lotus-crowned hailed with joy the festal days.
Golden lyres, sending forth rich, harmonious strains
Sounding the key-note, which o'er the world still
     reigned.
High above all, the Vestal's song enchanting soars,
Mingling with the ripples on the wave-washed shores.
From the Temple floats the bell's melodious chimes,
So deep and mellow in that old Atlantian time.

Throughout the Ages, linger these old memories still
And hover round me with no effort of my will.
Still in my heart is throbbing with the rythm of the
     waves,
Those slumbering waves which, alas, became our
     graves.
Again, I hear the glad hozannas to the Sun arise.
Isis in the sanctuary, is veiled from human eyes,
Which read no warning in the skies' celestial hue;
Nor heard it murmured in the Ocean calm and blue;
Neither listened to the whispering wind so free,
Telling of the doom, fair Atlantis was to see.

I am thankful that the gates of memory ope,
That great Angels weave the scattered threads of
     hope
And clothe us freshly with its robes of snowy white;
While on our altar shines again the mystic light,
The radiant star, which once o'er Egypt shone,
Glimmers once again, with a message all its own.
Humble tho' the Temple, the melody is there,
The bell's sweet chiming breaks upon the silent air,
Amid the incense rising from our sacred Shrine,
Old Atlantian glories round our spirits twine.

CHAPTER II.

THERE is yet a little more of the flotsam and jetsam upon the stormy waves of human unfoldment which is supplemental to our opening chapter, and must be detailed now or put entirely to one side. From two distinct sources, we give an account of an old Mexican city that has never been entered by the foot of a white man and which was known to be in existence long before the Spanish Conquest:

"Mr. Juan Alvarez, who has just returned from an exploring expedition in the southwestern part of the republic, reports that he has found a city which has never been entered by a white man, and which has evidently been in existence for hundreds of years, going back before the time of the conquest of the country by the Spaniards. It is an old Aztec city, and the approaches to it are so guarded by nature that it is an impossibility to reach it if the inhabitants do not want a traveler to get in.

The city lies in the almost inaccessible mountains in the extreme southwestern part of the country and is so far away from civilization that few white men have ever been in the neighborhood. It was by the purest accident that Alvarez became aware that a city was anywhere in the vicinity, and after he found it, all of his endeavors to reach it were unavailing on account of the persistent opposition of the natives.

He had been traveling over the mountains in search of an outlet to the Pacific Ocean when he came to the top of an elevated plateau and crossed to the further edge. He had a magnificent view, and while looking over the country, saw what he took to be houses in a far distant valley. A close inspection with a glass convinced him that what he saw was really a collection of houses, and he at once set about reaching the place to see who lived in that part of the country.

After days of hard work climbing over cliffs and mountains, he reached a point from which he obtained a good view of the city and saw that it was regularly laid out in streets and was peopled with a race who knew something about civilization. The houses were of stone and were surrounded by yards, in which were growing flowers and shrubs. On all sides were evidences of taste shown by the inhabitants, and it was evident that he had found a city which was not known to the outside world.

"A careful examination of the country showed him that the city was located within a natural amphitheater and was accessible from one side only. He saw that the only means of access was through a long and narrow defile which led into the mountains from the Pacific coast side, and he started to reach the place, where he could find this entrance. He made an outline drawing of the city as it appeared to him from the distant mountain top, and this is all he has to show that there is a city within the heart of the mountains, for he was never allowed to reach the spot.

"From this drawing it is plain that the city has not less than four thousand inhibitants The houses are all of stone and are supplied with doors and windows. In the center was a large building, which was undoubtedly the temple of worship, for on its walls could be seen sculptured designs representing the Deity. It was in the shape of the ancient teocalli, which are to be found in many parts of this country, and the people could be seen passing in and out of it during all hours of the day.

"After ten days' arduous work Alvarez found himself at the foot of the mountains on the western slope, and set about searching for the canyon leading to the city. He had so well marked the lay of the land that he had no diffi-culty in finding the entrance, but he was met by a band of Indians who refused to let him proceed.

They offered him no violence, but insisted that he should return. He told them that he had come over the mountains and did not know how to find his way back.

"After a consultation, he was told he would have to remain awhile as a prisoner, and two runners were sent into the mountains, who returned in a day with orders from some one in authority, and Alvarez was blindfolded and placed on the back of a mule. He traveled in this condition for three days, only having the bandage removed from his eyes at night.

On the fourth day, he was told to remove his bandage, and when he did so, he found himself on the borders of the Pacific Ocean. The Indians had gone, leaving him with nothing to guide him back to the place where he had seen the city."

This city is described in full in "Future Rulers of America," and has been visited by persons in the body, who have been permitted so to do.

We conclude our extracts with the description

of another mighty city, the work of the powerful nation whose capital, located on the great island of Atlantis, exercised its power both East and West, of which we are trying to tell:

"The American archaeologists who went to the recently discovered city in the Sierra Madre Mountains have returned, and tell of another hidden city five Spanish leagues north of the first city. The leader of the party, C. W. Pantion, of Philadelphia, says that these cities were evidently twin capitals of a wealthy district long before the Aztecs appeared. The two cities are connected by underground passages hewn out of solid rock, and it was while exploring one of these passages that the second was discovered. It lies in a deep basin of the mountains, with no exit except the underground tunnel. At least none has been found.

To that which we have thus drawn from all accessible sources in the visible, I now desire to add supplementary testimony from the Astral

Records, which I believe to be reliable and worthy of credence.

Does not this collated evidence of the similarity in nature and civilization west of the great city, which could not possibly have had commerce with the mother-country for centuries, prove conclusively, even to the realistic and scientific mind, a common origin for religious teachings, customs, languages, both oral and written? All the discoveries relative to this subject, confirm this conclusion. We are indebted to those who are impelled by an irresistible desire to learn and know. Who, in this cause are willing to expatriate themselves; endure danger and overcome obstructing difficulties, if they may but by some chance guidance, bring again to the light of day, some of the various records, which were left when the sun of the manifested spiritual world went down into the shuddering earth?

To the Aryan people, who listen with a willing heart, there is much that can be given concerning

this ancient city. It matters little how Science
and Religion shall accept that which is offered,
whether in a scientific way, or from the unseen as
true and of value. Science and Religion have
never received anything new upon untried lines
of thought, until they have been forced to the
exception.

That is why the priests, of all ages, are so conservative and have withheld so much more than
they should, even on their conservative line of
thought. It has ever been their rule, to hold fast
upon that of which they had become possessed;
content and satisfied without the trouble and
exertion of seeking new fields for themselves, or
admitting the possibility of broadening truth,
for others.

All that has ever been learned, to distinguish
the savage from civilization was known to the
wise men of Atlantis. Whenever there has been
upon the earth, a sufficient number of Atlantians,
at one time to control a nation, or to form one by

themselves, that nation or epoch has always ex-
perienced a most wonderful growth. In the days
of the last Egyptian splendor, when it was the
school to which the Greeks and Romans resorted
for instruction, was the last time noted in history
of such a re-appearance in sufficient numbers to
admit of a national control. What they did, we
have the pyramids; the Temple of Karnac; and
all the mighty ruins of the Nile and the Euphrates
in evidence.

As soon as the Anglo-Saxon speaking races
were sufficiently developed out of savagery, the
Atlantians, commenced re-appearing, startling
the whole world ever and anon, with their great
strides toward wisdom and knowledge, as they
slowly paved the way by conquest and discovery,
for the settlement and re-occupation of that which
belonged to them; and for the utilization of all
their old resources, under new conditions of added
strength and experience. In no other way can
we account for the wilting and extermination of

the red-skinned usurpers, who had neither claim nor strength to maintain title to that into which they had strayed by accident during the temporary absence of the real owners.

Much sympathy has been wasted on the red son of the forest. He has but obeyed the law: Who cannot dominate the resources of the environment must yield title to him who can. How much would our vast storehouses of mineral and agricultural wealth have helped man's unfoldment, if they had never been used? The difference between the American Indian and the Anglo-Saxon-Atlantian, is plain to the dullest intellect.

As the city of Atlantis grew, her population was drawn off into colonies which had deep and abiding influence on the whole of the Western continent, but especially centering along the belt in which Atlantis itself was located.

Between the fading away of the last Egyptian civilization, and the concealment of the world's records at that time, there is a mysterious gap, which can be accounted for only in one way. When Atlantis was in its prime, there were other units in the world's category of nations which were not so far advanced. If Atlantis had held on in the even tenor of her way, all other nations of the world would have received the light, and been uplifted to something near its own stand-point, but when this chance of development was cut off, they groped in comparative darkness. When this class of people incarnated again in force of numbers, such scenes as the conquest of Rome by the Goths and Vandals; the overrunning of Europe by the Huns, and the eruption of the Tartars, times without number, occurred. As they disappeared from the mortal vision, we can but recognize their sameness of purpose, and the most pertinent fact that undone duty made all this trouble for the Atlantians of the Far Past, their comrades and associates. Have we learned the lesson that no human being is separate from ourselves? A wrong once done must be righted. It is the eternal law of exact justice.

As these misbegotten *impedimenta* to progress pass out into the unseen, having overborne or put off all heads that towered above their own, intellectually, Atlantian influence revives. Little by little have these "fellows of ignorance," felt the uplifting of influence of the "sons of light" and every generation increases the widening wave of educated and spiritualized people, which must finally include within it every nation, tongue, or people of the earth's full complement of inhabitants. The American nation has done a vast deal for the enlightenment of the whole world. Thus it is easy to understand why the extinguishing power of all that holds the soul in chains is projected toward us.

In the ancient times, when the lamp of civilization burned at Rome, and Athens, or later, as at Antioch and other cities; single centers of learning blazed out and lessened the darkness as do

beacon lights set on a hill. But with these compare the events of to-day. A compact, unified
nationality, which resembles the old Atlantis, had
its beginning on an island, cut off from easy approach. Yet it has been able to make its power
felt throughout the whole world. Although the
English name be detested, its power is always re-
spected. Not only has this nation made itself
felt everywhere, but it is the founder of the
American nation and unites its force with that,
to push the common civilization and thought currents into every part of the globe.

The freedom of the thought-body, and the
aptitude of the minds engendered thereby, has
once more drawn to the American continent more
Atlantians than were ever incarnated at one time,
since the fall of that city. It thus happens that
their inventions and knowledge and wisdom and
the results of thought-force, modified and perfected by the assimilation of hundreds of years in
devachanic rest, is coming upon the nation in a

flood, as with outstretched hands they demand from the Silence that which they themselves deposited in the Astral records long ages since.

We often wonder at events transpiring in the way of discoveries, or at the applications of principles which are perfectly logical, and linked one upon another. We have surely reached a point and begun to guess about the uses and methods of application of that vehicle of force about which the Atlantians knew much, and desiring to know more, found there was a limit which barred their further progress. We already have hold upon another, and we desire only that they who may essay to advance in this direction, may do so with body, soul and mind so purified, they will not need the reprimand of obstruction, that came to the original investigators of our nation on that line.

The reason why this age is so celebrated above others of the near past, is due to the facts thus stated. We perceive in the near future, as has been repeatedly foretold, the end of a cycle is at hand. Cataclysmic results; the sinking of land in some places; and the rising in others, is imminent. When cities peculiarly situated are crowded with inhabitants, who have lost all conception of everything but their own desires centering in selfish purpose, their thought vibrations become inharmonious with the universal thought vibrations. If this inharmony continues strong enough to communicate itself to the ground upon which the city stands, this foundation being subject also, to a set of vibrations upon the natural plane of Liquidity, serious consequences may occur.

Just what the outcome of the present period will be none but the Council of the Seven Great Builders know. But this we have gathered: That within a hundred years, and possibly· a much shorter time, Atlantis will be above the waves. Whatever her monuments contain, or whatever may be in her ruined temple can then be investigated.

Within 500 years the bulk of population will be south of the equator; that which is now sea, will become dry land, and the old continent of Lamuria will once more sustain its millions of inhabitants. Scientists tell us that the time is fixed when all the gold, silver and coal will be mined. How short-sighted! Under the sea is a thousand-fold more than has ever been brought to light by man's busy hands.

CHAPTER III.

IN the early seventies, having by constant and
severe attention to business reached a
point when rest and change were imper-
ative, I was advised by my physician to take a
sea voyage. I mentioned this fact to a friend
of mine in New York City, who was a vessel
owner. He offered me the position of super-
cargo in one of his vessels about to sail for San
Francisco, "around the Horn." I gladly accepted the chance, for it gave me both motive
and occupation for the trip.

My preparations were made rapidly. We
sailed out of New York Harbor on the 15th of
June, 1872.

As the last lighthouse sank slowly beneath the
waves, and the full moon rose in the heavens, I
stood watching the receding land marks, little

dreaming of the momentous events to happen as
a part of the voyage, nor of the marvelous re-
vealings to come to my knowledge, before I
should again touch my foot upon land. Of all
these the following pages are but a feeble portrayal. But it is always so in life, we meet and
part, come and go. The consequence of the
meeting and the pain of the parting may be in-
expressible in spoken language; but how shall we
know? Who will tell, or warn us, of the swift-
ly oncoming future, with its burden of weal or
woe?

As our vessel was devoted to freight, we, as I
knew, carried but a single passenger, who by especial favor of the owner had been permitted to
occupy the one spare cabin. The rest of the
space was occupied by the officers of the ship, including myself. I had been introduced to this
man, when he had first come on board, but being much preconcerned about the business I had
in hand at that moment, I had simply responded

with the usual meaningless phrase of: "Happy to make your acquaintance." But I remembered afterwards an impression of dignity of hearing; of sweetness of real courtesy on his part; and that peculiar, indescribable thrill as we shook hands, which once or twice in a lifetime, it may be our good fortune to experience, as the lines of our lives cross with those who are essential to our highest and best unfolding.

Standing thus, leaning meditatively over the taffrail, I came back to myself by hearing my name pronounced distinctly, in a low, musical voice, with just the slightest foreign accent. Looking around, I acknowledged the address, as he went on to say ·

"I see you are leaving part of yourself behind you."

"Oh, not a large part," I replied, "but I was thinking about the certainty of parting and the uncertainty of meeting."

"Don't you think that we part forever from

our friends, only when we have accomplished
or finished all that we can do for each other.
So long as our work remains undone we shall
certainly meet again?"

"Yes," I said, "that may be so, but it is the
human uncertainty that saddens."

Looking full at this man, to whom, with his
every word, I was most indescribably attracted,
I saw a picture, from that time indelibly stamped
upon my memory. Tall, and almost perfectly
proportioned. Eyes black, while in their ordi-
narily kind expression, one might easily imagine their possibilities, when honest indignation or
righteous anger stirred their depths. Hair and
beard white, and worn a little longer than custom prescribed. His bearing was majestic in
strength; serene in harmony; attractive beyond
compare in its unselfish desire for the good of
others. With all this, there was an impression, in all he said, he could tell very much more
if he only would, about any subject concerning

which he might be conversing.

It was such a face as children love and scoundrels hate, containing within itself the pitying tenderness of a mother's love and a father's sustaining watchfulness. In our interview, I passed from the outermost border of casual acquaintance to the confident championship of sworn friendship. At this, too, I marveled, for I am slow to receive or offer friendship, but come slowly to the perception of what might be, in those who honor me with their good will.

Although we stood some little time longer gazing upon the ocean, as the night and waters met in closer and still closer embrace, we lapsed into silence, with that strange feeling of being company for each other, although no word was said, and finally we descended to our respective cabins for the night.

As is usual with the position which I held, my duties during the voyage were almost nominal, making up for this leisure, however, during the receiving or discharging of the cargo or any part. Consequently I had sufficient time to improve the acquaintance so curiously begun. It did not take long to find out that my friend was a zealous, unremitting student, and that while we were familiar with many lines of common interest, there were others, in which he was well versed, of which I knew comparatively nothing. He was a very eloquent and instructive talker and readily and gladly answered my questions.

Especially was this true of things in the past, which the present generation has moved on and forgotten, and a peculiarity of his descriptions was that they were given as if personal experiences of his own. Later I knew why, but at the first it seemed that it was done to give more life and movement to the story.

As a child I had always been fascinated with whatever I had chanced upon, either in reading or conversation which related to Atlantis. But as I grew older, enveloped in the materialistic ideas of the modern schools, I had come to regard the little that was known of that ancient mistress of the seas as largely fabulous, if not wholly unworthy of credence.

After we had been out from port four or five days, as we sat chatting on the quarter deck, something was said which induced me to ask him the question squarely:

"Do you believe there ever was such a country as Atlantis?"

"Most certainly," was his quiet, decisive answer.

"But you do not think it possible that a whole continent could disappear so utterly beneath the waves as that is said to have done, leaving no more trace of its former existence than has been the case with that?"

"And why does this seem impossible to you? Does history know anything of the city that stood under ancient Troy. Who knows who were the builders or what the design of the Pyramids of Egypt? Who can tell of the cities lying strata upon strata in the valley of the Nile? In your own country, who can tell anything of the Mound Builders? What does the world know of Palmyra, of Babylon, or of the great cities in the Valley of the Euphrates? But for the accessibility of their ruins, they would by this time have been as thoroughly forgotten as Atlantis now is."

"And," here his face softened with an infinite pity, "perhaps within forty years from now we may have another lesson in the opportunity for denying the existence of the past."

"But maybe," he continued, "you would like to hear some of the actual records brought down even to your day, of an event that concerns so intimately every living person now upon our planet."

Upon my eager assent he went into his cabin and soon returned with a small black-letter volume, written after the style of the Far East, upon parchment, from right to left. Opening it he read in his sweetly modulated tones, translating as he read, the following extract:

"Facing the Pillars of Hercules was an island larger than Africa and Europe put together. Beside this main island there were many other smaller ones, so that it was easy to cross from one to another as far as the further continent. This land was indeed a continent, and the sea was the real ocean in comparison to which "The Sea" of the Greeks was but a bay with a narrow mouth.

"In the Atlantic island a powerful federation of Kings was formed, who subdued the larger island itself and many of the smaller islands and also parts of the further continent. They also reduced Africa within the Straits as far as Egypt, and Europe as far as Tyrrhenia. Farther aggression, however, was stopped by the heroic action of the then inhabitants of Attica, who, taking the lead of the oppressed States, finally secured liberty to all who dwelt within the Pillars of Hercules. Subsequently, both races were destroyed by mighty cataclysms, which brought destruction in a single day and night. The natural features of the Attic land were entirely changed and the Atlantic island sank bodily beneath the waves.

"In the center of the Atlantic Island was a fair and beautiful plain. In the center of this plain and nearly six miles from its confines was a low range of hills. Here dwelt for many generations the renowned race of Atlan, from whom the whole island and sea were named Atlantic or Atlantis. The ruling Kings ever handed down the succession of power to their eldest sons, the younger sons going into the priesthood. They were possessed of such wealth as no dynasty ever yet obtained or will easily procure hereafter. This wealth was drawn both from all foreign nations with whom the Atlantians traded and from Atlantis itself, which was especially rich in minerals, and possessed the only known mines of orichalcum in the world, a mineral with most wonderful and inexhaustible properties—a metal which was then second only to gold in its value.

"The country was rich also in timber and pasturage. Moreover, there were vast numbers of elephants, spices, gums and odorous plants of every description; flowers, fruit trees and vegetables of all kinds, and many other luxurious products which this wonderful Continent, owing to its beneficent climate, brought forth. These were sacred, beautiful, curious and infinite in number. Nor were the inhabitants content with simply the natural advantages of their glorious country, but also displayed a marvelous industry and skill in engineering and the constructive arts. For, in the center of the island they built a royal palace, every succeeding King trying to surpass his predecessor in adorning and adding to the building, so that it struck all be-holders with the greatest admiration.

"They cut about the Royal Palace a series of waterways or canals. These were bridged over at intervals, while an immense canal admitted the largest vessels from the sea, giving at once protection as a harbor, and making it more convenient for the transportation of freight to and from the interior. In fashioning their interior streams they left docks cut out of the solid rock where their triremes could land their cargoes.

"The stone used in their building was of three colors, white, black and red, so that many of the buildings presented a gay appearance. Their walls were covered with brass (which they used like plaster), tin and orichalcum, which had a glittering appearance.

"Northeast of the center of the Continent, stood the great Temple. The interior was covered with silver, except the pediments and pinnacles, which were lined with gold. Within, the roof was a magnificent mosaic of gold, ivory and orichalcum, and all walls, pillars and pavements were covered with orichalcum.

"By a system of aqueducts leading from natural springs of hot and cold water, they had supplies for baths, and for the irrigation of their beautiful plantations and gardens.

"The docks were filled with shipping and naval stores of every description known to men at that time. The whole city teemed with a dense population. The main canal and largest harbor were crowded with merchant shipping returned from, or making ready to sail for, all parts of the world. The din and tumult of their commerce continued all day long, and the night through as well. Such is a general sketch of their wonderful city.

"Now, as regards the rest of the country; it was very mountainous with exceedingly precipitous coasts, and the plain surrounding the city was itself environed by a mountain chain broken only at the sea entrance. The plain was smooth and level and of an oblong shape, lying North and South. The mountains were said to be the grandest in the world for their number, size and beauty. The whole country was a constant succession of prosperous and wealthy villages, for there was an abundance of rivers and lakes, meadows and pasturage for all kinds of cattle and quantities of timber. They surrounded this plain with an enormous canal or dike, 101 feet deep, 606 feet broad and 1,250 miles in length. By it the water from the mountains was conducted around the whole plain, and while a part flowed out to the sea, the rest was husbanded for irrigation. They were able, by raising two crops a year, to double their productive capacity.

"In the polity of the Atlantians the Kings maintained an autocracy and the priesthood were their council of consultation in all matters of State, until at last the power passed into the hands of the priesthood.

"For many generations, the rulers, King and priest remained obedient to their ancestral traditions. For they possessed true and altogether lofty ideas and exercised mildness and practical wisdom, both in the ordinary vicissitudes of life and in their mutual relations. They looked above everything except virtue. They considered things present of small importance, and contentedly bore their weight of riches as a burden. Nor were they intoxicated with luxury, but clearly perceived that wealth and possessions are increased by mutual friendship and the practice of true virtue; whereas, by a too anxious pursuit of riches the possessions themselves are corrupted and friendship also perishes therewith. Thus it was they reached the great height of prosperity we have described.

"But when, at the last, their mortal natures began seeking to dominate and override the Divine within and about them, they commenced to display unbecoming conduct, and to degenerate; thus blighting and finally destroying the fairest of their most valuable possessions."

"This," said my friend, "is as authentic an account as that of any nation of whom we have any history, for it was handed down from father to son in the ancient Atlantian writing, which was perfected about 25,000 years before the Christian era commenced.'

Just then some duty claimed my immediate attention and as he rose up to return to his cabin he looked me fully in the face and remarked: "If I mistake not, the time is close at hand when your desire for information on these lines will be more fully gratified.

CHAPTER IV

IT was a day or two before we had a chance for any more conversation, for he seemed to be very busy in his own cabin with what looked like an ancient map and a number of diagrams of cabalistic calculations, which I fully recognized, for I had some experience with researches along that line, and could, to a certain extent, verify some of the simpler rules of deductions from the Caballa. But, as I could see, the operations upon which he was engaged were very complex and far reaching and concerned some of the mightiest secrets of planetary creation.

I also noticed while the problems seemed very abstruse and complicated, he did not seem at a loss in any sense, or puzzled. His absorption being the result rather of the length of the process.

At last he appeared to have reached a favorable conclusion and his data and memoranda were put away. Once more he came upon deck. Although for a few days he apparently put aside a continuation of his former talk about Atlantis, yet there was an uplifted expression of content, lending an added charm to the ever-restful dignity of the perfect face.

While he had been thus busy it had occurred to me I had an odd volume in my locker I had picked up in a second-hand stall in Boston, intending to examine it at my leisure. Now, having my interest aroused I brought it out and found among much that was quite discursive, the following pertinent paragraphs:

"The fourth Continent, which it has been agreed to call Atlantis, was formed by the coalescence of many islands and peninsulas that were upheaved in the ordinary course of evolution and became ultimately the true home of the great race known as the Atlantians, a race developed from a nucleus of Northern Lemurians, centered, generally speaking, towards a point of land in what is now the mid-Atlantic Ocean.

"In connection with the Continent of Atlantis we should bear in mind that the account which has come down to us through the old Greek writers contains a confusion of statements, some of them referring to the great Continent as a whole, and others to the last, small island of Posidonis. Plato, for instance, condensed the whole history of the Continent of Atlantis, covering several millions of years into an event, he located upon the island of Poseidonis (about as large as Ireland); whereas, the priests spoke always of Atlantis as a continent as large as Europe and Africa put together. Homer speaks of the Atlantes and their island. The Atlantes and the Atlantides of mythology are based upon the Atlantes and Atlantides of history. The story of Atlas gives clearly to us the clue. Atlas is the personification in a single symbol of the combined continents of Lemuria and Atlantis. The poets attribute to Atlas, as to Proteus, a superior wisdom and a universal knowledge, and especially *a thorough acquaintance with the depths of the ocean;* because both continents having borne races instructed by divine masters, were each transferred to the bottom of the seas, where they now slumber until the appointed time shall come to reappear above the waters. And as both Lemuria, destroyed by submarine fires, and Atlantis submerger by the waves, perished in the ocean depths, Atlas is said to have been compelled to leave the surface of the earth and join his father Iapetus in the depths of Tartarus.

"Atlas then personifies a continent in the West, said to support heaven and earth at once; that is, the feet of the giants tread the earth while his shoulders support the sky, an allusion to the gigantic peaks of the ancient continents, Mount Atlas and the Teneriffe Peak. These two dwarfed relics of the two lost continents were thrice as lofty during the day of Lemuria and twice as high in that of Atlantis. Atlas was an inaccessible island peak in the days of Lemuria, when the African Continent had not yet been raised.

"Lemuria should no more be confounded with the Atlantis Continent than Europe with America. Both sank and were drowned with their high civilizations and 'gods,' yet between the two two catastrophes a period of about 700,000 years elapsed.

"Why should not your geologists bear in mind that under the continents explored and fathomed by them, in the bowels of which they have found the Eocene age, there may be hidden deep in the unfathomable ocean beds, other and far older continents whose strata have never been geologically explored, and that they may some day upset their present theories."

Amazed at this singular corroboration of what

my friend had previously read me, I concluded I would ask him something more about it, at the first opportunity, not dreaming that the opportunity of lives was close at hand.

During all this time we had been making good time toward the South. Both officers and men had been attracted toward our passenger, and all were ready to give him the little attentions which make a stranger feel at home anywhere. I mention this as explanatory of some events which happened a little later.

The winds had been brisk and favorable, but as we approached the Spanish Main they grew fitful, and when we had traversed a part of that West Indian Archipelago, they fell away into a dead calm. Our ship drifted a little to the South, but made no particular headway. On the third day, the moon fulled at noon and we were lying in about 30 degrees North latitude and 42 degrees West longitude, when my friend asked me if I would like to go with him to visit a peculiar looking island, about a couple of miles to the westward. Upon my rather eager assent, the captain granted us the use of his yawl, and though he proffered us the help of some of the crew, our friend declined, saying he had been much accustomed to the water.

We pushed off, I taking a pair of oars and he steering. I had hardly taken a couple of strokes with the oars, when I felt that the rapid impulsion of the boat was not due to my strength. I glanced at my companion. His face was set with a peculiar expression, of which I had before had experience in other directions.

A very short time sufficed to bring us to this island, which on closer inspection seemed to be the summit of some huge obelisk or pillar, a little raised above the waves. The sides, although not high, were sheer and precipitous. In the still waters they extended below the surface, as far as vision could penetrate. How much farther, I had no means of ascertaining. We rowed slowly around it. It was about 150 feet in circumference. On the side farthest from the vessel the face of the rock was broken jaggedly by the weather. The projections gave opportunity for fastening the yawl, and for climbing to the summit. If there had been any swell of the ocean even this would have been impossible, but with a sea of glass all about us it was not a very difficult task. Having securely knotted the boat's painter to a stout protuberance, we scrambled as best we might to the top.

To my utter surprise, instead of the flat, solid mass, roughened by the weather, which I expected to find, it was cup-shaped in the center, evidently filling with water during storms, and drying out under the hot sun. It was now dry at the bottom. Looking closely at the sides I saw that instead of being a mass of natural rock, it was a structure built of masonry by cunning hands, so perfectly and solidly as to defy, thus far, the fierce action of the most erosive forces of nature. The floor was laid in regular flagging. Almost stunned by the discovery, I turned to my companion, but my exclamation of surprise was checked by his actions. Standing erect, in the very center, with his face to the North, guiding himself by a small compass and a little square of parchment, upon which characters were inscribed, he turned 15 degrees to the East and stepped forward one pace. Then turning 15 degrees more he stepped forward another pace. He repeated this operation until he faced due East. There standing erct, his form seemed to dilate, and his face grew fixed and set in its whole outline. All at once I perceived a large disc of stone had revolved at his feet, exposing a flight of stone steps leading into a room below. Coming back to himself he motioned me to follow him, and slowly we descended the stairs into an ante-room below, opening into a larger room. As we stepped upon this floor a light which came from nowhere in particular, lighted up the whole

interior. Limitless age had laid his desecrating
hand upon everything. But as this had been her-
metically sealed by the waves, the   dust `that
would otherwise have accumulated in the upper
air was not present. In the center of the room
were five stone seats, on each was a little pile
of dust. My companion, still silent, stepped to
the East, and facing the seats, made one of the
signs of Power. As he did so I thought I heard
a suppressed sob of joy, but it was not distinct
enough to be unmistakable. Then going to the
exact opposite side of the wall, which was par-
titioned into a series of curious entablatures, he
touched   some   mechanism,   which,   preserved
through the ages, obeyed the will of this wonderful man. A door slid back, through which
we passed into a chamber below. Here we
found seven seats. On each rested those curious
little piles of dust. My friend repeated the sign
made in the room above, and then a sound like
the tremor of an Eolian harp rose in volume un-

til the vibration filling the room, shook the walls of the tower in which we were standing. Turning to the Eastern face of the wall, from a niche therein he drew out a little stone box. Holding this carefully, he retraced his steps towards the upper air, closely followed by myself. With the greatest care he closed behind him every avenue, thus sealing once more for future unfolding, whatever there might be of knowledge or mystery here concealed. When the disc at the top had rolled into its place, a roll of pigment was placed in his hand by unseen helpers. With this he traced upon the tightly joined edges a character which burst into a silvery flame as it appeared, upon the stone, and left a blood-red mark behind it. Then proceeding to the side where the boat lay waiting for us, we managed without any difficulty to seat ourselves in it and push off, he steering, as before.

Singular as it may seem, without any preconcerted instruction or word of warning, not a word had been interchanged between us from the moment of our landing until we were again in motion upon the water. On my part the silence was involuntary. I seemed to stand in a vortex of recurring memory, coming down overwhelmingly upon me. I was too busy within myself in attempting to readjust the past, the present and the promises of the future, to leave any time for the frivolity of speech. I could not resist the feeling that these rock-ribbed chambers were, in some peculiar way, a part of myself. I knew I had been perfectly familiar with the purposes of their erection, their use, and of some final issue, appalling and benumbing in its effect. More than that. The five seats of the upper chamber and the seven seats of the lower, to my inner vision, were filled with an occupant, shadowy, but so distinct I could recognize the features, as one recalls the lineaments of a long absent friend. Then came the names as if I had parted with them only yesterday. Oh,

Memory the Eternal! was it yesterday, or thousands of years ago since I looked upon these faces and forms of comrades loving and true? The feeling of present reality, of some tie stronger than friendship overwhelmed me. When my friend made the sign I mentioned, a burden of untold weight was lifted from my shoulders, as if an expiation were finished, a terrible mistake rectified whose consequence all my life, up to that hour, had cramped and restrained all my unfolding and its energies. All this and much more that words will utterly fail to portray, held me silent as my friend did, what he evidently came to do, taking me as an involuntary accomplice.

Sitting in the stern of the boat, facing me, with the stone casket resting on his knees, he looked at me with a grave smile, and said:

"My brother: I see my confidence in thee was not founded in simple assumption, but in knowledge. Thou hast learned well the lesson whose closing clause is to keep silent. Thereby thou hast proved also thy position in the Great Brotherhood, whose first charter was issued by the Atlantian Kings. I greet thee, Ancient Wise One."

While saying this his whole face lighted up as if from an inner fire. The action of the sympathetic exaltation on myself was beyond the power of words to describe. It was as if one had suddenly come to a perception of almost infinite power, and without a particle of arrogance in the possession. I could only reply:

"I feel that we must have been brothers, but you do me great honor in naming me thus."

"Before we reach the ship I must tell you," continued my comrade, "that it has been permitted you for purpose, to revisit the tower of the Great Temple of Atlantis, in which were gathered for concentration during the last awful cataclysm which sent the continent beneath the waters all the living members of the most potent Brotherhood that has ever existed.

"You entered the chambers of the three, the five and the seven. The whole continent is slowly rising once more. The top of the tower, which was 100 feet in diameter at the base, and 210 feet high, has again reached the upper air. The transparent dome, which covered the chamber of the three has been destroyed by the action of the waves. We do not know whether the masonry of the upper stories will be able to resist the erosion of fierce tropical storms or not, as little by little it reaches the surface.

"It was thought best by the Brotherhood to rescue this;" here he touched the little casket, "before it might be overwhelmed and forever hidden by the insatiable maw of the waters. It contains the fullest continuous record of the last years of our once glorious country, at present accessible.

"The chambers which we entered were built perfectly air and water-tight, and for that reason have preserved their contents to the present time. Below the last chamber we entered was that of the fifteen, and still below that, the chamber of the forty-five. I did not enter them, for I was warned that I might thereby afford opportunity for the waters pressing up from below, to wipe out all vestiges of this ancient home of the Brotherhood, which to later generations may be ocular demonstration of our existence.

"Obligation rested heavily on the three, the five and the seven. They could not be set free entirely from its responsibility until such time as either the bounds were destroyed, as in the upper chamber, or one clothed with authority entering their resting place should give them their signal of release, which I did. Below the seven, the failure of conditions above absolved the members of the remaining chambers, and they were set free in a very short time after the cataclysm.

"You are well known to me as to the rest of

the Ancient Brotherhood, and have been chosen again as in the long ago past, to be the spokesman of our beloved Order, in its newest appeal to mankind, and we are sure that mistakes of the intellect in the past will not be repeated in the present. But we are approaching the ship. The most important object of our voyage, the possession of these records, which no person living or dead could obtain without your actual presence in the flesh is accomplished. The voyage was planned and undertaken for this purpose, and will result as planned. Our vessel has been lying over the entrance to the great port, at the mouth draining the Atlantian Continent, from which, before the overthrow, a magnificent panorama of the fairest land the sun ever shone on, was visible.

"We could not accomplish our object until near the full moon, so the calm has lasted until this time. But to-night as the sun goes down a breeze will spring up, and by to-morrow our voyage will be moving rapidly forward to its completion."

It did not occur to me, during all this recital, to object either to the facts stated or to the certain, quiet assumption of myself as one of the willing accessories of the plan he had thus hastily sketched. It seemed quite a matter of course that the sole object of my making this voyage was the accomplishment of what I now, with mortal ears, for the first time heard. Nay, more, I felt a certain enthusiasm, a quiet joy in being thus permitted to do the task, whatever it might be that was set for me, as an integral factor of the whole, to complete. I know that this is not at all the thing likely to happen, according to deduction from what we know of human nature. But as this story is one of facts on new lines, we cannot be guided by precedents, or the working of known laws; as we seek rather in the fields of the unexplained laws of nature, for a solution of the phenomena presented.

But we were now close to the ship and the men were making ready to hoist the yawl aboard. As we reached the deck my friend showed his casket, as a curious souvenir of the stone pile we had visited. After looking at it casually they assented to the fact: "It was a nice bit of rock, looks a trifle water-worn though." And so, knowledge of incalculable value passed beyond their reach, forever; or at the least, until the refiner's furnace of the ages shall have prepared them more fully for the perception of that which may at any time be offered them.

CHAPTER V

A S the sun sank on the Western horizon a northeastern wind began to strain out our "idly flapping sails," and the good ship once more moved merrily over the waters.

The full moon of the tropics climbed out of the great wastes of waters, and my friend and I sat on the quarter-deck, chatting of various matters. Suddenly, as if some one had spoken to him in reminder of some event, he said; "Yes, certainly; at once."

A moment after, the stone casket which I had seen in his cabin just before sunset, was put into his hands, coming about as fast as a man would walk, out of the companion way. At that time no one else was near us on the deck, therefore no remarks were made.

In my peculiar state of mind this, too, seemed

perfectly natural, as well as what followed.

Taking the casket in his hands he pointed out to me several characters and symbols engraved deeply in the stone. Calling my attention to a form of the winged globe, he said: "That is the signet seal of him who was our most learned, Ancient Brother. It holds the contents of the casket in trust for him who hath the password. Let us see if we may open it.

"Lay the open palm of your left hand on mine, the fingers straight, and say as thou mayest receive out of the silence. If thou art he whom I have expected to meet, it is well. If not, then it is still only patience for further waiting."

He held out his left hand, palm up. I placed my own left hand upon it, palm to palm. As I did so, a little shock passed over my whole body like an electric thrill, only a little more intense. His eye shining with a piercing brilliancy, caught mine. Then I felt another hand lying on the back of mine, and a form shadowed out of the

thin air by my side, and simultaneously I could
see the full, regal proportions of a most majestic
figure standing beside us. Prominently out of
the shadow, as when one feels the sun's rays, I
could distinctly feel the brightness of another
pair of eyes similar to those of my friend in the
body.

At the same moment of time there came ringing through the air to my ears a low, musical
chant. Instantly I appeared to be up-borne
where beneath me a vast city lay spread out, in
all its beauty and glory for many leagues. We
three still remained together in the same relative
position. I had lost all consciousness of any difference of condition in the three present, who
seemed equal in every respect. At this instant,
a single syllable from my friend's lips, indescribable in its intonation, arrested my attention.
Without volition of my lower consciousness, in
exactly the same cadence I uttered a syllable, and
then, like the soft, clear ringing of a silver bell,

thrilled from the lips of our bodyless brother, the third syllable of a word whose awful powers all mystics concede.

As the last note rang out into space the casket came once more fully into my consciousness. I saw it open slowly, until the cover turned fully back, and revealed a large roll of the finest papyrus, clearly written in plain but minute characters of what we have supposed was a transition period of Egyptian civilization.

My friend reverently raised the scroll from its resting place. As he did so a fragrance inimitable and of bewildering effect upon the senses poured from it. Holding this precious record of the past in his hands he said:

"For over 29,000 years, my brother, this papyrus has not seen the light. When it was last inclosed in this casket and sealed, we three, still in the body, looked forward to the accomplishment of much that was beyond the power of limited mortal potency. I am glad to greet thee, my companion and brother. I was not mistaken in thee, for to no power but the presence of the three would the casket have yielded its contents. When I shall have read it to you it will be left in your hands for safe keeping. To-morrow we will begin our work, giving six of the early hours of the day to it."

CHAPTER VI.

S O on the next morning we commenced our tale of transfer and rescription. He translated while I wrote down in short-hand that which he thus gave me. At the first it was slowly given, owing to the fact of my being a little rusty in my stenography, but as I recalled my skill, our speed increased.

The MSS. was a full and complete record of all that concerned that wonderful country, whose daring leaders, like many another seeking to manifest unusual power, have come in contact with impassible limitations and pulled down their country and involved all in irretrievable disaster, because they lacked omnipotence to carry out their designs. But I will not anticipate, but submit to my readers the history of Atlantis and the story of the secret causes that led to the final overthrow, as I have copied it from the notes of that never-to-be-forgotten voyage. It begins with an invocation by the Scribe, as follows:

"I, Tlana, Scribe of the Mighty Three, to whom it has been given strictly in charge so to do, herein write the history of my beloved country. This is to be for the instruction and enlightenment of my people, when they, in the **far** off ages to come shall need more than bread, help to recurring memory. I demand for this undertaking, the necessary assistance and guidance from the Brotherhood of both the Invisible and the Visible, so soon to become of the Invisible; from the gods of Wisdom and Power, and from the Supreme Ruler of All, that I may say that which is best and most instructive concerning the actions and conditions of our nation from its beginning to now. (About 29,000 B. C.)

"Our Continent follows the general outline of all the others now in manifestation upon **the**

Earth. It is about 1,000 miles broad at its widest point, and 3,000 miles long at its longest dimension. The surface is mostly level, consisting of vast fertile plains. But to the West, North and East the country becomes mountainous. From these mountains, as a water shed, a river with its branches drains nearly the whole length of the Continent. Its waters, diverted through an artificial canal and locks, forms the great port of the City of Atlantis, which extends from this canal, northeast of the central portion of the continent, quite up to the foothills of the elevated portion of the country. Among these mountains has been built the Great Temple dedicated to OM., who is the ONE, the All.

"Our records fail to give us any information of the beginning of man's occupancy here, and it is only through the power of perception of our wise men that we gain any idea, of that beginning. It is sufficient to say, when the Fifth Race men needed a home for their unfolding, they found it here. Their unfolding has been along the lines of the strongest development. We may therefore simply describe the conditions now existing as the outcome of the thought-forces of the most powerful nation of the known world.

"The fertility of our soil is unparalleled anywhere upon the earth. Our difference of elevation above the sea level gives variety to our climate, and whatever grows otherwhithers on the globe, will grow here also, in the greatest luxuriance and perfection. We have no need to import anything grown out of the ground from other nations.

"Our supplies of minerals from the bosom of the earth are incomparable in their amount and abundance. We have all metals found anywhere upon the surface of the earth. We also have one, of which none has ever been discovered in any other country. It possesses the ductility and color of copper and the strength of iron. We have named it Orichalcum.

"The fauna holds every species of animal, which from here has been carried to all parts of the earth, there to find a new habitat and become of use to the children of men either for labor or pleasure. This was the center of distribution. Whatever knowledge or wisdom on this line experience has given them, they have freely passed it on to those who stood in need of it. In short, whatever mankind possesses in any degree anywhere, we also possess in vast abundance, far beyond our needs. Never has any State, Nation or Potentate ever before concentrated so much of wealth; that is, surplus of supplies of all kinds, as we hold to-day.

"No word but immense, will truly describe our public works. No nation has even dreamed of a Temple like ours, much less built one. The private residences of our citizens, even of the poorer sort, outshine in beauty of design and suitableness of material the kings of many other nations. Do not consider that I am seeking to belittle others or to extol ourselves, but I am stating as fully and as candidly as I can, that which is really the fact, as I now write.

"The mountains have springs of hot and cold water which act as natural reservoirs. From them the water is conveyed by stone pipes to the public baths and to the private residences of such citizens as choose to avail themselves of the privilege under certain conditions.

"In the center of the city are the royal palaces, and these are protected by three immense canals, which are built entirely around them, with two intervening zones of land. These canals are connected with the Great Sea by another canal 300 feet wide and 100 feet deep and six miles long to connect with the port.

"The Great Temple is in the northeast part of the city. Its lofty tower bearing upon its top, the finest observatory ever yet built, occupies the northeast quarter of the Temple grounds. This and the Temple itself is protected from attack on the North, East and West by the mountains, which serve both as a defense and a foundation to hold up the massive structures built upon them.

"From the mountains the city of cities extends in a circular form southward. Beyond the immense area occupied by the city proper is still another, comprising upwards of 75,000 square miles, which has been cultivated from time immemorial, and is in fact one vast garden. This is liberally irrigated from the river and from a canal 600 feet in width and 100 feet deep, extending through the country 1,200 miles. Not only are these waters used for irrigation, but through a system of locks at the port, galleys are raised and lowered into the grand canal, where they both receive and distribute cargoes of all kinds of products in the interests of commerce.

"It is hardly necessary to mention that **the** population of this plain and the mountains **is** many millions. Never will there be so **many** people gathered in the same place at the same time, so say our prophets and Magi.

"Nor must I forget to say that the volume of our population is increased by the fact that owing to the dominance of the life-giving power of the spirit, which has not been weakened yet to any great extent there are three or four generations of men upon the earth at the same time, all strong and vigorous. As the necessary supplies for the maintenance of the body at its best, are in the greatest profusion, nature in no sense retards the increase of population, but would support to the utmost limit the most prolific increase possible.

"During the day the myriad sounds of voice and action that arise over the docks and the quarters of the city devoted to labor is like the roar of a tornado on the sea, hurling itself against the embattled rocks.

"The Atlantian galleys have reached every port and nation under the whole broad heaven.

They have laid the entire surface of earth under tribute to our commerce. We have no need to ask another nation for anything we have not. But they seek from us the fruits of our soil and our incomparable bronze manufactures, in whose production our artizans have become very expert, especially in clubs, axes, knives and swords.

"The barbarians of the Eastern world have never been able to make these things for themselves, and as the material and tempering of our artizans are very fine, we find market for all we can possibly offer. The only article of which we fail in making the supply equal to the demand is a bright yellow metal, which offers a powerful resistance to the action of the elements. It is eagerly sought for purposes of decoration, both of building and persons. The total product of our own mines is thus appropriated, and our traders have discovered that it exists in other parts of the world. So they seek it everywhere, and when found offer our own products in exchange for it. When they bring it home they are offered certain immunities and privileges in addition to the market value for it. Thus, in a way, it has become a measure of value, not only with us, but with all the nations of the earth. It is predicted by our Magi that this peculiar condition, through the foul greed of man, will grow into a calamity for the whole race. The desire upon which its gathering by us is founded will become irrepressible and destructive in the more physical nations in the years to come. As, however, our nation has done no intentional wrong and have tried to deal justly, they can hardly be considered responsible for any such evil. It is also true that if evil does come upon the race we shall be forced to meet it in the long ages yet to come, as we are again called to face in new bodies the lives allotted to us. Thus far, strained intensity for acquisition has not acquired force enough to injure us in our development on any line.

"We are not a nation of flesheasters, for the warmth of our climate does not compel the concentration of food sought in the use of flesh. It is because we are not bound to the soil in our efforts to overcome the circle of necessity that we can give so much time to the study of the real forces and facts of the universe, and the methods by which they could be made useful to themselves.

"At the North are three high mountain peaks, which have become landmarks for all seafaring men. In the way of review of what I have written, permit me to take my future readers to the highest summit of the great peak Alyhlo, and from thence point out the paradise of mountain and valley, hill and plain, interspersed with broad plateaux. These are covered with tropical vegetation bearing all kinds of edible fruits known to man throughout the whole circle of the year. Limped streams from the mountain sides water a large portion of this vast district.

"Nor is this all, for the whole picture is dotted thick with substantial dwellings, hamlets and towns. But above all, is the capital as a center of interest, and an exchange of thought, so wide, so far-reaching, that all the other centers in the whole country seem but suburbs.

"Notice also the varied greens of the vegetation and the blue of the sky, so clear and so perfect, as yet undisturbed in its vibrations by the shock of either offense or defense. Beyond these can be seen the canal leading to the land-locked sea and the great port with its fleets of arriving and departing galleys from every quarter of the globe. These galleys move neither by sail nor oar, nor any impulsion of elemental force. Surmounting all these our Magi have imparted the secret of etheric impulse born of thought, and against this, wind nor tide have no power. It is the fairest land that man in all his generations thus far has ever seen.

CHAPTER VII.

BEFORE going forward with the description of the MSS. let us do a little comparing with the present situation, as we now know it. The location of the Ancient Continent must have covered in part the Carribean Archipelago. If the land were so raised as to make the highest peak six miles high, there must have resulted two immense inland seas where now is the Gulf of Mexico. Across these and the old continent would blow in constant succession the trade winds, bringing moisture and fertility upon their broad wings, for the teeming population. In configuration, there must have been a striking resemblance to our upper lake country.

The range of mountains to the West and

North must have constituted the backbone of
the Continent, whose peaks and table lands now
form a chain of islands. On the line of drainage
from the inland sea the Amazon must now be
located The fertility must have been the result not so much of a torrid temperature, as of
the absence of cold winds, which gave a peculiar,
equable, life-developing climate, both for vegetables and animals. Everything possible grew,
because there were no drawbacks to its growth.
It was always seedtime; it was always harvest.
Bud, blossom and fruit in all their different stages
of maturity could be seen growing at once on
the same tree. What is partially true to-day
of the orange and lemon was then true of all
fruit-bearing trees. So fertile was the original
condition of the soil, and so great the wisdom
of those who directed, that the matter of planting
seed and gathering harvest became a matter of
sequence and not of season. With this explanation let us return to our manuscript:

"The change of condition from life to death is one accepted and welcomed by our people; not in any sense feared, because during their long continued existence the monotony of physical life is fully satisfied and the only inducement for accepting prolongation is the increasing of the spirit's force and potency, with which we are well acquainted and fully educated as to its limitless possibilities.

"Our place as carriers for the world, has for many years been acknowledged. On all seas and in every port are the galleys that supply the world's marts, flying the Atlantian flag—a winged globe in blue on a yellow ground. It therefore happens in our ample harbor, the myriad swarms of shipping, although loaded with the products of the whole earth are ours.

"The sailors of other nations dare not move out into the vast wastes of waters, separating the different countries one from another.

"Great warehouses lie along the water's edge,

which is bordered from the sea, for many miles into the interior, by immense, solidly-built walls. These are raised high enough to be above any high-water mark of either flood from the interior or tide from the ocean. But floods were rather the result of changes in the amount of drainage, for the melting of snow on the mountains or increase of amount from suddenly precipitated vapor, was a thing of but slight importance.

"The capital is connected with all parts of the kingdom by iron tramways, upon which enormous loads are moved by a motive force, whose secret only our Magi know. But the obedient force moves back and forth, drawing and pushing, as it is bidden by its controller, the heavily ladden wagons, to which it is harnessed.

"The whole city is built of a pure white marble, taken from quarrries in the Northern Hills, whose supplies are used not only for building at home, but also for export. So fine is the grain and so elegant the polish that the blocks are used over and over in rebuilding in the cities of the Mediterranean. This stone cannot endure the extremes of temperature of the Northern climate, but is amply strong for all that may be demanded under an Atlantian sky.

"From what I have already said, perhaps it will be plain, the city is laid out like a disc, with a segment wanting, where it is fitted against the foothills of the Northern mountain ranges.

"Broad avenues in semi-circle begin at the mountains and end in the mountains. These are crossed at regular intervals by other avenues, forming the radii of the circle, the center of which is the King's palace. There is no ownership of land, save in the King's name as the representative of the nation. It is held by our Magi, that no man can own anything in which his own labor, or some representative thereof, does not constitute a component part. All articles of handiwork therefore can be claimed by the contributors thereto, but man has not, and can never attain, ownership in the four great elements of manifestation—fire, air, water, earth. If he ever shall attempt it, disaster and degradation will attend the attempt. If a man builds a house or plants a tree, or cultives a crop, then the house or tree or harvest belong to him, and he should be protected in his right to enjoy fully, all that can come from his labor.

"All lands are parceled out by lot, and the improvements only, have a price. He who would like his neighbor's location must, with his neighbor's consent, buy the improvements, but the land has no more value than the air about it.

"The houses are built for convenience and comfort. Every family owns its own home, and when a young man takes to himself a wife, he has a portion of land assigned him, under conditions which make equable all inequalities of place, quality or surroundings. No crowding is allowed, not even in the thickest part of the city. The buildings are of permanent material, fashioned to let in the air and light. The underlying principle is a central open court, with the living rooms all about it. This plan is modified in many ways to suit the individualities and needs of the owners.

"The court is entered by a broad gate, swinging easily on its ample fittings. In the center a pool with an overflowing fountain to prevent stagnation, cools the air and helps modify the vibrations. The water was supplied by an acqueduct from the mountains. This was so old that no Atlantian of the present people can give its age. But there are records in the archives of the Temple concerning the planning of the huge undertaking and the manner of its accomplishment. About this pool the building stands, generally two stories, so supported on pillars, as to form no obstruction to free movement of the air.

"When the young couple decide to locate it is the custom to receive from the chief astrologer of the Temple a horoscope definitely naming the number of the new family to come. For each one a room was built in the home. This special allotment prevents crowding, and is productive to the utmost, of progress and growth on all lines.

"Animals herd, man individualizes in his tendency. At either end of the scale, acceptation of, or rebellion against the herding, indicates where he stands at any given time, as regards either his spiritual or his physical nature. If he is inclined to be brutish it matters not if fifty hands eating with his, dip into the same bowl of porridge. If he is spiritually unfolded he would prefer to appropriate and use, in his own way, that which comes belonging to and prepared especially for himself. This is not, as it might at the outset appear, selfishness, but is the outcropping of the work which the Ego takes upon itself during the earth lives, the soul-building out of the incarnations.

"The rooms on the first story are larger and

mostly used for the offices of living, in which the family relations are concerned and perfected. Most of their leisure time is spent about the fountain in the court, where there are always agreeable shadows, with the blue sky above. The courts are paved in colored patterns with a kind of glass, and carpeted with rugs and mats woven from vegetable textiles and fancifully dyed. These goods are made principally for export. Besides these furnishings, there are side by side, products of man's thought from every part of the earth, the richest and the best. None are blood-stained as the spoils of war, for our traffic, industrious and honorable has made us beyond peradventure the richest nation that ever existed upon the earth.

"From the first, we have traded everywhere. No galley of ours has ever been seized by the god of the seas and left lying upon the ocean bottom whether bearing our goods forth or bringing back to us the merchandize of other lands. This natural increase by labor and by trade, without loss, should of itself have been sufficient to have enriched us without other means

"Thus it is perceived the families are by themselves, each is an independent community. Their houses and gardens are as much the kingdom of that community as can possibly be conceived. This is the rule of the spiritual and not of the physical.

"But I must not forget to speak of the streets and roads of the city proper and the outlying country. These are laid out on a certain general plan, which once established has never been changed. Although they have been many years in construction and extension, every foot has been added under the direction of a master mind in conformity to a uniform plan adopted thousands of years ago. So far as they are extended they are finished and lasting. The substance used for the road beds is our secret, of the whole world. Our ways are dustless and noiseless. The peculiar composition readily yields traction to bodies moving over them. Never has there been so perfect a system of easy transportation upon the earth.

"The public buildings are always large, roomy and of varied styles, surmounted with domes, pinnacles and minnarets and ornamented with statutes of artistic design and workmanship. The material of which these are built is white marble. Atlantis can well claim not only the honor of being so created, but of remaining a white city. There is no darkening effluvium in the air nor the climate to obscure the white walls set in the great billows of surrounding green. Our Magi say, that in days to come, a nation on the Mediterranean Sea called the Greeks, will personify in their works of art, our beloved city as a beautiful woman rising from the sea.

"The more important of these buildings are profusely decorated with gold, and it is for this purpose that metal is so eagerly bought by the Atlantian traders, a poetical name—'the tears of the sun,' has been adopted by our people, and by this it is most widely called here. Of the palace of the King; of the Great Temple, I will speak more at length by and by.

"In these public buildings are rooms for social meetings, to discuss public topics and for the convenience of classes studying things that do not belong to the physical plane. A description of one will be a description of the general plan of all. They are elliptical in form, with a fountain in the center. The Atlantians are extravagantly fond of the presence of water. At one of the foci are a number of seats, arranged like an amphitheater, built of stone and rising one above another. At the other of the foci stands a Tribune, upon which the speaker stands when public addresses are made. About the fountain also are seats, where the auditors sit easily and converse one with another.

"In like manner are built the training schools of the young; the central part of the structure being open to the sunlight and the air. Here the young Atlantians are educated in the things that belong to the nation, the family and to themselves. Our fathers had a saying we seek to make a rule of living: 'Eight years to infancy and play, eight years to boyhood and training in physical things, eight years to young manhood and learning of the world outside of Atlantis, and one thousand years to learning of the invisible and real.' Its proportions are very nearly correct.

CHAPTER VIII.

THE Atlantians of either sex are almost perfect in their physical organizations. They are nearly all equally trained by the master of wisdom. It may be asked why they are not all on the same plane of development. The reply is the conclusive answer of all ages and times. Man never has and never will exercise his individual potency in exactly the same way. The little variation, hardly perceptible at first, is increased by every increment, no matter how small, of each of the succeeding lives. This difference is increased also by the force of intellectual power which comes to a nation and of necessity to the individuals of the nation, who will seek to occupy the best bodies and positions, as the returning egos claim place in the lives.

"Because of the absolute equality of the sexes the bodies of the women are just as strong and vigorous as those of the men. But we know that in other nations, with which we have come in contact, in other parts of the world, the women are inferior in size and strength. This happens because the people of those nations have allowed themselves from generation to generation, and from age to age, to believe in and assert the inferiority of women. This continued thought has belittled and dwarfed her, not only in body, but has also bound her aspirations and her mental capacity with bonds stronger than steel. While the barbarian races, to their sorrow and loss, have made this sad mistake, the Atlantian nation, on the other hand, have constantly held to the equality of the sexes. The result now is, physically, both sexes are models which painter or sculptor are proud and eager to copy. Each one is a specimen of beauty, for perfection is beauty. The action of the climate and transmitted principles have brought intellectual vigor and daring with a marvelous grasp of perception upon the laws of nature and of themselves. Their bodies, instead of being impediments to spiritual growth and advancement, are helps indeed to the spirits who seek through them experience, knowledge and understanding. Those who might be called the common class, doing the necessary labor of the nation, are far advanced beyond the literary class of the barbarian nations in their perception of the truth and their knowledge of nature's laws. The day will come in the future when men will mourn this knowledge forgotten, when the fatigue and monotony of burden bearing will be almost overwhelming in its crushing awfulness.

"We have schools for the development of the physical and for the directing of the mental habits of thought. In these schools very little memorized knowledge is imparted. The design is to so train the faculties that if desired or needed the cipher of the Astral books could easily be read.

"Sickness is unknown. We have no lame, halt, blind, deaf nor dumb, nor beggars as models for maternal pre-natal mind, to misform embryos, and thus build monstrosities for the public charge. This of which I speak is true of the nations who are busy in the affairs of commerce, of agriculture, or who are builders and decorators of houses and public buildings. But there are some who from natural impulsion have sought more and more of the invisible, of the truths which belong to the ONE, and those who rest in IT. These are willing and anxious to devote themselves and their powers constantly to obtaining and attaining, and the teaching of youth. The only class distinction we have is founded upon knowledge.

"It has come to pass in a natural fashion that these thinkers have gravitated toward one another; that they have kept records of observation, experiment and experience; that they are wiser in speech; in mathematics as applied to the unseen; in alchemy, in astrology, and they are specially wise in the physics which embrace the laws of the unseen. At first buildings were set apart for these students and their teachers. As the city grew each body of students had its building, now known as temples. Later, all were gathered into the one great Temple, in order that the symbolism of the ONE who is ALL might be perfect.

"In the teachings of our Magi, all manifestation, on all planes, is referred back to the ONE, as the single central source of strength and power for everything obtained and obtainable. Thus the mind dwelling on this thought has striven in design, in material, in finishing and furnishing to make the Great Temple a perfected symbol of the ONE. Its worship in all its imagery and suggestion combines every element for the impressiveness of mode and subject, under discussion upon the minds of the student. Is it any wonder that there has come to us as a nation a deep-seated veneration for the Omnipotent name and laws.

"It is also a fact that our Magi are in possession of most wonderful powers, in the control of elemental forces who obey their will, coming to their tasks, not under confinement, but because obedient to the will and behest of those who call singly or unitedly for their services. It is also known that this power never will be held except by Atlantian born people, regardless of the changing conditions of the globe.

"It is also true that a far greater proportion of our people have attained to the superior light and knowledge than any other nation upon the earth either in the past or present. This is doubtless due to the fact that our incarnating egos, having the right of choice, have again and again sought their own people as the most privileged spot in which to make advancement during the lives.

"When these advanced egoes have found their bodies we have the spectacle of children born old, for the brightness of the last life is heavy on them, and the newness of the body does not always act as a defense or shield from its imperious blaze. It is not in each, but is a matter of ordinary, detailed development.

CHAPTER IX.

W E have but one basic law throughout
the whole country and city. It is
called the 'golden rule,' or preference
of another before self. We have no evils aris-
ing out of the action of selfishness, for this condition is the primary result of the fear of desti-
tution, either for ourselves or others, sometime
during the position or period of earth-life. Even
they who are the least advanced understand from
our teaching the true idea of Brotherhood; that
no man, no man's wife, no man's children, can,
under the law, suffer from deprivation of the
necessities of physical life. He who has more
than enough is held to be always the steward in
trust for him who temporarily has less than
enough. But this does not relieve from the ne-

cessity for labor, of every individual in the direct ratio of their ability, at whatever employment they are best fitted.

"In the building of our houses, the quarrying of the stones, the transportation and the fitting is all done by elemental force, under the direction of a master, who is in charge of a section. It is his duty to educate them and to see that they are duly provided for, out of the Astral storehouse, by the power given into his hands. The form of government has already been copied from us by a powerful nation in the Northern part of Asia, but because of their situation on the physical plane, it is most likely they will be able to retain only the form, and will lose the spiritual power which is the foundation and potent principle.

The whole nation is linked together by the master of the families, these are in groups and classes, under instruction and direction from those who are most competent to teach. These teachers are grouped under the masters or Magi of the Temple. These Magi of the Temple are under the instruction of the Most Ancient, the Seven, the Five and the Three. So, in the hands of the Three, mightiest of all human intellects, rests the destinies, the prosperity and the happiness of the whole nation. Moreover, upon them as directors and arbiters, the responsibility of Karmic conditions rested, as they were engendered by the currents of potency issuing from themselves and returning upon their cycle bore with them, whatever had been impressed upon, or mingled with them during their revolvment among those to whom the currents were sent.

"It must be apparent, to whom this MSS. may come, that the power of the Unseen, and their application to man's earth-life are matters of the greatest interest and importance to the Atlantians. There is no temporal power, save as a symbol of the Manifested. Everything pertaining to organized effort originates with, and is

carried forward by the Priesthood of the Great
Temple, which represents the dominant power
over matter of the spirit at its highest and best.
They have specially in charge the study and development of all occult knowledge.

"Every house is independent of itself. The
Atlantians are Monogamists—the one husband
of one wife. This, experience has demonstrated
to be the best condition for the development of
a strong, spiritual race. We have seen that
polygamist races always decrease in power,
strength and energy of purpose.

"In Atlantis, to be diseased or crippled in
body, or to be at the head of a family, in which
is such a member, is deemed a crime against the
people. Therefore all thought, all desire and
interest are brought to bear upon physical conditions, through occult and spiritual forces, not
only to make the nation whole, but whole in
the highest and best sense.

"Those who are particularly gifted with

psychic qualities or whose spirits have attained familiarity with the instrument intrusted to their hands are trained for the offices of Masters or Guides. These may or may not have families, but in either case, they are persons to whom a certain number of persons or families look for council, advice and guidance.

"For thousands of years have the Magi of the Temple, who give their whole time to the study of the Unseen, and lay aside their bodies at their own volition, really placed the welfare and best good of the people beyond any other consideration whatever. The nation is happy. They have no poor. They have no inferior class. All necessary labor is honorable. Generation after generation, we have been growing stronger and more like the gods come down to earth. We have perfect communication with the outside world and each other. We know Atlantis is the fairest city on this planet, and we are content.

CHAPTER X.

HAVING thus far advanced in the description of the most wonderful city ever known to man, permit me to quote from the words of one who saw what he so fluently and graphically describes for you:

"To the Northeast of this island Continent is located the Great Temple, built both for use and symbolism. On a plateau of many acres in extent, where the gradually rising ground began to break into the foothills, the whole surface had been leveled and paved with some soft material, of which the Atlantians alone knew the secret. This hardened under the action of the sun and atmosphere, until it was like adamant. To the East, a belt of country reaching to the seacoast, but not on a level with it, had also been

smoothed and paved, so that there was no obstruction to the eye, until it rested on the far-off
horizon.

"Upon this broad expanse of level space, close
enough to the mountains to be buttressed by their
mighty arms, stood the great, white-walled Temple, facing the South, and the ample areas for
assemblage. The closed courts and offices, and
the cloisters of the Temple faced the mountains
of the North, and thus secured for the Temple
Dwellers the privacy needed for the Masters
and student Brotherhoods of the Temple, who
were seeking to know out of the Silence.

"The Temple proper consists of two stories,
the first one consisting of pillars springing from
the rocky foundations of the mountain and supporting arches, which in turn, held up immense
slabs of stone, the floors of the second story. On
the first floor there is little or no inclosure, but
within the walls of the second story it is all arranged for privacy and quiet thought. He who

looks over the battlements of the upper story, looks down about ninety feet, into the beautifully paved court below. On the East and West of the Temple itself, are gardens, groves of trees, fountains, running streams of water, domesticated animals; and flowers of every hue and fragrance. These are sacred to the Temple, but open to the people under the surveillance of the caretakers, except certain reserved spots close to the Temple, which are for the special use of the students and teachers. In the northeast section of the Temple building was the great tower and observatory, fifty feet in diameter, rising 210 feet, a landmark and light extending hundreds of miles and ever a joy-inspirer for the sea-tossed mariners of the State.

"Looking from the plaza in front, toward the interior of the Temple, its vast recesses, its forests of white pillars and its high-lifted over-arching roof fills the spectator with awe. Nor was this feeling lessened by the cleanliness, the continuous shifting of huge masses of sunlight and shadow, ever into new and indescribable grotesquerie. During the services the awful solemnity evoked was of a character that modified the whole Atlantian thought and national purpose.

"The great tower was commenced fifteen feet below the surface. The original trap rock was supplemented by a square block of concrete rock, and upon this was carried up the superstructure to a total height of 225 feet, the square of fifteen. Upon the floor of the Temple resting on a raised dais was the secret chamber of the Holy of Holies. Across and through this, at High Festivals, blazed and flashed the Veil of Isis. Above, on a level with the upper floor, was the chamber of the Forty-five, and still above that the chambers of the Fifteen, the Seven, the Five and the Three. In the outer, the Tower was smooth and unpenetrated on its surface from bottom to top. It resembled a solid block, chiseled out of quarries and set on end, so deft was the workmanship and so perfect the jointings and finish.

"In the cloisters and rooms of the second story of the Temple were the apartments for private study and class instruction. There were also supplemental apartments, hollowed out of the neighboring mountains and reached by secret passages so arranged that whatever should be deposited in them as treasuries would be securely held, even if buried beneath the surface of the sea for ages.

"Beyond the great plaza, toward the city, trees and fountains shaded and beautified clear up to the naked edge of the vast pavement."

This is a faint portrayal of that which was really the culmination and concentration of the Nation's thousands of years of existence and unfolding.

"In all our Temples, and more especially in the Great Temple, the outer courts were but the simple separation from those who have no inspiration for the inner and higher. In the outermost court, or court of the people, were always gathered those who had thoughts of their own, and who were undecided as to what direction they should take in pursuit of the light slowly dawning upon them.

"The inner court of the people contained those who have so far perceived, that they are willing to obligate themselves to carry out certain purposes, of whose full intent they can know but little, except that the farther end is lost in the light of life, and the halo of obligation. In this court they who seek must be fitted by training and preparation for that which lies before them, so it is natural that they who linger there, striving to advance, must do whatever they can through their own power of assimilation, by themselves.

"At the first, if the lesson is concentration, it is their individual concentration. If the lesson

is passivity, it is their own individual passivity.
It is exactly as when one is learning to sing, as a
beginning, the voice is trained to use its own peculiar function alone. After this solitary practice, when some aptitude has been attained and
a facility of use, then they are ready for the
massing of singles for a united effort. It must
follow then, that the outer court of the Brotherhood cannot but lap over into the inner court
of the Temple.

"That which is done singly and alone, is absolutely necessary for the next step in advance,
which is to be made in unison with another or
others, in the same way as musical students are
trained by twos and fours for united efforts of
action and harmony.

"The question considered in all this is, how
shall growth and attainment be best accomplished? What is the basic principle?

"In music we say the sounds are set to a certain key, and however prolonged the action of the

vibrations, the key .and time will be the same, and,
all the vibrations are aligned. It is exactly thus,
when the students come to act together on the
occult planes, the vibrations which they produce,
will not, of course, be alike, but they must chord;
the parts of one vibration fitting and filling in
with the vibrations of another, so there shall be.
no jangle.

"To get the best results it is always best that
they who are in the outer court of the Brotherhood should be watchful and careful lest the vibrations sent forth from themselves should be
hastened or intensified or even drag through, the
thoughtlessness of their own carelessness.

"When once. unity of action is attempted in
this matter, it is absolutely necessary to success,
that the key on which they start should remain
the same.

"It is easy to see how intense passions, such
as anger, or any of the disturbing conditions
would interfere with the vibrations. It would be

like a chord out of tune in a stringed instrument, where, though the strings do not give out
the same sounds, still they must be in alignment.
This alignment is the source of all music.

"It is not needful that the most intense feel-
ings of one's nature should be given rein, and allowed to make disturbance, both for himself and
those whom he is contracting. It is also, on a
small scale, like the sharping and flatting at the
wrong points, whereby the vibrations are
changed, the harmony broken and discord becomes perceptible.

"It is also absolutely necessary that all conditions in the outer which can cause a disturbance
should be held in abeyance, when one desires to
concentrate, in order that during a united effort
for concentration the harmony and strength shall
not be marred. This is true of all work on any
occult line.

"It is not to be supposed when two or more
of the Brothers are concentrating, exactly the

same process is gone through within the mind of each. That would be impossible. The end sought for can be attained by each working in his own way, with the same thought. It does not follow because A does not perform his task exactly as B does, that B should set up a disturbance in the vibration as reflected from A, thus in a measure destroying the co-operation and effect to be produced.

"The law of the Temple then, is first, alone; second, in company with those who are seeking by united force to accomplish, as the Masters of Destiny, at all times, have been able to accomplish. Unity of action is most important, therefore we must guard against anything that can disturb this unity. If vibrations, in their normal conditions lay along side by side, and one is hastened, then the harmony is destroyed and the action of the impulse is to increase the vibrations in the length of their wave force. We must, when meeting for united effort, insist that each for themselves, shall become their own guardians. Knowing that disagreeable things will occur, we must be ever prepared, at once, to **put** them aside. Having done this once, we shall **be** stronger to continue. Thus the music from our soul's action will not only affect ourselves, but those about us.

"Upon this statement of principles has been built the great law of the Temple: 'Do unto others as you would have them do unto you.' All the teaching and training, all the ceremonies and symbolism of the Temple are founded upon this law as the corner-stone of the religion of our people. Having given this brief summary of the truths, our priesthood have in charge, let us pass on to a description of some of the ceremonies of the Temple service, and, as an illustration, we will take the Great Feast of the New Year, as more fully including the whole, than any other.

"The feast of the New Year, on the 21st of March, consummated and commemorated the

Sun's re-birth! when, out of equal days and nights a new Spring and Summer began for the northern hemisphere, and the promise of seed-time and harvest was renewed.

"At this celebration it is expected that every family in the kingdom should be present, either personally or represented by some member of the family. All the going and coming of the year is planned with this in view. It is considered a privilege for all the outlying population to be made welcome in the capital at this time. The feast lasts seven days.

"Let me attempt to describe at length, for no pen can truly portray all the wonders of that marvelous assemblage, one of the last feasts which took place, ten years before the destruction of the city. The government and people were at that time in their most perfect unity.

"About three days before the set date of the feast there could be noticed a little stir of preparation all over the country. It was a quiet

movement toward participation. If one had
been lifted above, so he could have looked upon
the continent as upon a map, there would have
been perceived during these three days, long lines
of travelers, some on foot, and others by every
method of conveyance, moving upon the city in
converging lines. As the time grew shorter the
extent of these lines grew shorter and the ways
close to the city and in the city itself were filled
to overflowing. There were but few people in
the outlying country who had not some friend
or relative in the city proper. When the houses
were filled, tents were spread in the gardens,
and in all the parks and places of assembly. Thus
there was a new appearance given to the light
by its reflection from the tents, which were some
of linen and some of cotton, but all bleached very
white by a process known only to the Atlantians
and never imparted to any other nationality.
Only on the great plateau of the Temple and
the areas of the outer courts, no tents were al-

lowed, for that space was necessarily kept clear, that there might be room for the greater assembly.

"As the ceremonies were in commemoration of the new-born sun, the hours of assembly were morning and evening, and at the moment of the meridian height. On the first day of the feast, as the dawn brightened in the East, out of the early twilight, there could be heard throughout the whole city a low, muffled sound like the pouring of a swift torrent through a smooth bed, and as soon as it was light enough to see all the outer courts and the great plateau of the Temple could be perceived, crowded with those who had arrived to take part in the inauguration ceremonies. Their faces were turned toward the East, between whose far horizon and the eyes of the numberless watchers no obstruction intervened.

"When the moment approaches for the appearance of the Ruler of the Day, a low, sweet harmony, sounding in rythmic change, welled out

upon the air in slow, restful time and far-reaching tones, from the great Temple choir, who were
gathered in one of the porches of the Temple, so
raised as to be seen by all the vast multitude. As
the. sounds of the chant gradually swelled by the
voices. of the worshippers, became more intense
in power and heavier in volume, all the vast multitude seemed to sway, under the psychic spell
of this invocation to the Sun; this symbol of welcome to one who returns to his work and purpose. The minutes move quickly on, the invocation is finished, a blast of trumpets accompany-
ing the final note; the orb of day, with tropical
suddenness springs from his bed beneath the sea.
As his first beams fall upon the countless multitude, they drop upon their knees. With bowed
heads, in silent adoration, they ascribe all glory,
all power, all praise to that which stands to them
as the manifested source of life, of health, of
strength, the ever sleepless eye of the One. Then
they separate. The hours are spent in social con-

verse, or the abandonment of rest and quiet until it is high noon.

"As the Sun approaches the meridian, all the streets and byways, all the housetops, in all places where there may be a worshipper, behold his face turned towards the Temple. At the moment of meridian altitude, above the highest pinnacle, a crystal ball, almost as dazzling in its brilliancy as the sun itself, shoots up, and for a few moments receives the concentrated thought of all the faithful throughout the city, as the reminder of the good messenger of the One, the heighth of whose glory is now perceived. Again, in the evening there is a convocation at the Temple. The ceremonies of the morning are repeated, with the exception that the song is one of 'farewell;' the multiude facing the West instead of the East, and the hushing sounds of stringed instruments attend his exit from the Western horizon.

"These ceremonies are continued for six days.

There are various other ceremonies which take up the time of portions of the Convocation, between these assemblies of the whole. There are also lines of Temple services, work and study. Each of the sciences having its appropriate place and each being developed by those who are allied in the great Brotherhood of the Temple. This embraced the whole people in its ramifications. It is not necessary to describe these in all their minutiae. But during these six days there was continually something taking place in the city, always having its moving force at the Temple. The moving of a procession through the streets, a convening of the Temple guides or guards, lectures and talks from those who were so well qualified to give forth from full fountains to the inner souls, eager to be fed. But as the evening draws on after the waning of the sixth day, once more, all the courts of the Temple were thronged. The hum of conversation dies away as the darkness grows more and more intense.

"Now, when it shall have become quite dark, the Temple Choir opens the exercises with the song of invocation. It differs from all the music of the Convocation, hitherto, in key, rythm and time. In this all the people join. As the sound vibrates in swelling cadence, rising and falling amongst the echoing mountains, the effect was perfectly indescribable, for the Atlantians were especially celebrated for being sweet singers. When the singing was finished the chief instructor of the people stood upon a Tribune high raised, and there discoursed of the things which concerned them most intimately in the physical life; of whatever they stood most in need; of how the Sun was to them life and health, and plenty and peace, the sign and representative of all good. Then he directed their attention to the darkness, which sat so uneasily upon them, enforcing rest and inability to work. Then his peroration was after this fashion:

"The darkness is death and desolation, and

thus, in the beginning, the Existent saw, when he said: 'Let there be, and there was, light.' At this word millions of lights gleamed out all over the Temple, inside, outside, even on the highest points. It stood forth one blaze of white marble glory, for there was only one thing about electricity the Atlantians do not know, that is the point where knowledge lays hold with potency upon the One, in its inmost and supreme integrity of existence.

"There are other ceremonies of minor importance, pertaining to the night, but this is the most important. There are no sacrifices, no shedding of the blood of animal or human victims. The Atlantians do not believe it is necessary to teach destruction or destructive action by such sacrifice, in the burning or destroying of any living thing, for they say man is naturally destructive and we ought to teach him the opposite. So all our ceremonies lacked the hideous shadow of agony and horror, that will be sure to come if man forgets our teachings. But the great object lessons served well their purpose in elevating the whole people to the same level, and cementing them into a common Brotherhood. In the next chapter I will describe as well as I may, the last great day of the Feast.

CHAPTER XI

T HAT of which I am now to speak concerns the Atlantian nation when there was for it seemingly nothing more beyond, in glory, prosperity or knowledge. I am warned of the Unseen not to write unguardedly, but with circumspection, lest there come power for mischief, to the unobligated.

"In the olden days, when step by step we had painfully and laboriously climbed the mountain heights into the broad blaze of the everlasting truth, the world lay at our feet. That was our intellectual and physical status. Whatever there was in the earth itself worth having or knowing was in our possession as the birthright of ages and ages of previous existence.

"Furthermore, we coming into life are not clouded, as the generations to come will be, by physical conditions which will grow thicker and heavier all along the pathway of the unrolling centuries. It will be because, having dominated whatsoever there may be of physical workings, we shall have sought also to master that which belongs only to the spiritual realm, that we shall be cut off. There is but one God. None created can sit in the seat of the uncreated. None who exist by the thought of the Infinite One can hope to explain that which is of itself the Existent, the Cause of all results manifested or unmanifested.

"In the first part of the development of the Atlantian nation all communication was carried on by outer sense vibration, even as now. Perhaps the vibrations were not as intense as at the present. But in the latter days they who are instructed are taught by thought transference.

"The education of the young is not along the

line of simple memorizing. **Nor** is it only the unfolding of partially physical senses. It does not appeal to material sense for the building of the soul. We do not hope that out of bodily conditions we can bring any help to the spiritual. For we know whatever belongs to and lies along the line of the physical, rising to the highest source within itself can rise no higher than that point. More than that, the physical in its most perfect form begets weakness and death. How can there be anything beyond this but weakness and death?

"This is one of our axiomatic doctrines. In manifestation we simply see an exemplification of that which occurred on the spiritual plane.

"In the days to come the professor of mathematics will state an axiom or a proposition, and then going to the blackboard, and upon it, appealing to the sense of sight, will demonstrate in manifestation the impression he seeks to make, of the secret workings of the force beyond. If he is a chemist he will bring before his hearers certain elements, and out of the unions of these elements, out of the separation of the conditions, there will grow up or manifest themselves, certain, perhaps, startling conditions. But that which then takes place is not the truth he is trying to prove; it is simply a demonstration of the truth. Nor is the professor of mathematics trying to show you the truth. He will simply be trying to prove that to be true which he has learned from the physical side.

"Do not confound that which is unmanifested, with the manifested. The unmanifested is the cause of everything manifested. The manifested exists because the unmanifested is its primal cause, reaching down through all the ages. So we do not in these days linger over demonstrations, or in any way try to prove by simple manifestation the existence of the invisible and unmanifested.

"But the first course of training our students

receive is a line of strengthening for their mentality. If there are those who are so physically constituted that the machinery of their thought, the power by which they could receive of the force outside of themselves, is in any way unfit or incompetent, they are first treated by the thought of those who are about them, to bring them up into a healthful condition, as it is termed, on the physical plane. Really the condition is simply one of harmony."

The knowledge which has come in these latter days, to us who have the pleasure of perusing this manuscript, variously named "the science of spiritual conditions—mental science—science of truth —science of knowing"—call it what you will, is really a glimpse gotten hold of, by one who was clear-sighted and who, in the development of the idea, has manifested the bravery of the old soul. It is only to these old souls are intrusted the works that will stir every man's heart that hears of them. It is, however, by standing before the world and demonstrating for years and years, that which is the germ-cell of a most wonderful knowledge, the unfolding along invisible and spiritual lines can be accomplished. But I must not forget to state that the privilege of giving out these truths, so that they can be understood belongs to the Atlantian-born.

If these stand in their places to-day and declare their personal knowledge to be truth, until that truth is recognized, they have done for themselves a service—it matters not whether the clouds and thick darkness may inclose them afterwards. That portion of the truth which they have put forth will stand forever and forever. So what we know as an occasional matter of healing after a miraculous fashion was a thing of every-day occurrence with the Old Atlantians. Those who united for the purpose of increasing the race mated themselves first, according to the best knowledge belonging to the astrologers of those days. Thus mated, it rarely happened as

one of our poets hath sung: "Deformed, **unfin-**
ished, sent before my time into this breathing
world, scarce half-made up," was the fate of **any**
one born of woman. When any unripeness of
this kind appeared, it **was** treated success**fully**
on the mental plane.

CHAPTER XII.

THE students came together in classes, or small assemblies to hear and learn of the Wise Ones. The Wise Ones did not undertake to talk to the outer physical senses as I am talking to you to-day, but through thought-transference, that more vigorous and permeating condition, which some day, some of you will perceive and know, and this whole nation, so largely Atlantian, will come into the full possession of. Not only could the subject intended to be taught be fully and completely received, but with more intensity and a broader wave action on the plane of intellect, than you now receive.

Suppose, as has been said to you, in this day,

while we listened delightedly, it were possible
to give to a class of students, by asking them to
sit still a few moments, a demonstration of the
vibrations of color, sound or other sensed vibration, that lies just beyond. If I, as a professor,
and you as a class, sit listening eagerly, and I say
to you: "Sit still for a moment, turn inward your
consciousness and perceive," then I could by the
force of thought directed by my own mentality
make visible to you the quiet, the peace, the harmony that always does, and must, attend **the in**-
ner vision—how much time it would save; **how**
much better you would remember it, than now,
when you have to formulate within your **own**
brains the words symbolyzing the vibrations
which I poorly convey to you, and which no **two**
of you can conceive or perceive exactly alike.
This was our intellectually exceptional and brilliant mental training.

Whoever was particularly bright, desirous to
know of all truth, whose eyes turning to **the**

great, white tower, lifting itself aloft above our Temple, wished within themselves that some day within its shadow they might learn more of these things, were always sure to have the opportunity. When this eventful time came and the gateway was opened wide, there came also the obligation for fulfilling even as the obligations come to-day.

That which a master of the later day said: "A new commandment give I unto you, that ye love one another," was the inspiration, the thought and the most intense dictum of those who taught in the Temple. There must be perfect unity, perfect harmony, perfect love for one another. Oh, that you of this latter day had never forgotten, you who have remembered and put in practice all the commandments of the "dreadful ten," concerning the physical, would only recall and practice the Eleventh. Then all that could be needed in the visible life would come.

Seek ye first the knowledge and potency of the

Unseen in the realm of Truth and there will come to you knowledge of all else." The knowledge of the physical cannot be so very much. It lies along the contemplation of a few simple, foundamental principles. It is not so difficult to make gold as might be considered. It is not so difficult to do various other things which have come to our knowledge. Every step you have climbed along the way, which seemed so **difficult** at its first contemplation, after it has been accomplished, grew easier with the added knowledge.

Our records in stone, contained in the great treasury of the waters, hold embodied fundamental principles as established truths, which many earnest souls groping in search along the higher lines to discover, would give years of their own lives to know. Some of these, sooner or later, will come into knowledge. Those willing to advance, to expend the time necessary, to make the sacrifices and take upon themselves the obligation which must rest upon the consciences of all who are admitted to participation in the truths world-wide in the scope of their action, are candidates for knowing and understanding. They will certainly advance beyond the three-fold gates into the great mysteries.

That which belonged to the Atlantians as a nation intellectually and morally was the control of all knowledge, except that which belonged to the origin and power of life. This concerns the One alone.

Some of you whom I knew as men in the olden days, I now perceive as women. But the spirit that lies behind each one of you is the same; the perception that looks out of the eyes is the same perception that looked out of the body or dress you wore then, thousands of years ago. Oh, if you of this day and generation could only understand and perceive the treachery of the physical embrace, how the enwrapping into the physical is only a manifestation for the processes of accomplishment. If the experiences can come only through the body of a man, it takes that. If the object of the coming back into the lives can only be accomplished through the body of a woman, it accepts that, with its modicum of joy and terrible burdens of pain and mad agony on all planes. The body is nothing! The soul of the Ego is everything.

CHAPTER XIII.

IT was a doctrine of the Atlantians that the body of the physical which enwraps us, is adapted to the need of the Ego holding it, as a manifestation of the processes of accomplishment. If the ego coming back into the lives cannot accomplish its own unfolding, save through some particular experience, it compasses that particular experience, if it is within its possibilities. From age to age, from generation to generation, that which stands behind all, is ever the same. That which overshadows all is a part of the Divine Existence, is one with the One—a part of the Divine Existence, indivisible and always the same. This was the primary knowledge, taught first in the forests, amid the rocks and mountains; and afterwards in the Great Temple builded into these mountains. It must be remembered that very much of the work done in the Temple was accomplished by the control of the elements or elemental forces, which the Brotherhood understood and exercised even in those far off days, for the lightening of the toil of the physical. This, you in this day and generation have somewhat recovered. But instead of saying to the force universal, do this, you chain some portion of it, and bring it under limitation of form. These limitations act for you, tirelessly toiling day and night. And so, there does not come out of the surrounding conditions and vibrations the reacting powers and forces which generally tend to the physical retarding of any great building or other work of importance, because they are made up of the groans and moans of those who toil in the physical body to accomplish.

When elemental force builds, it builds because of its forcefulness, and there is nothing to retard. In no sense is there anything for regret or reparation. There are no tears, there are no

blood marks anywhere throughout the whole
work. It is clean. It is set in motion and directed by the force which originates in the potency of man the created, who thus becomes a
connecting link with the potency of the One who
manifested as the Universe.

In the northeastern part of the Continent was
a group of rocky mountains. These rocks
reached far down beneath the ordinary level of
the soil. They seem to have been buttressed up,
apparently from the very center of the earth itself, but that it was not so, appeared **by** the
future events. But in any event they **were** strong
enough to hold tons upon tons of piled up **rock** in
whatever shape it might appear.

So, first the rocks were cut down to a level,
and a huge plaza was thus cleared from east **to**
west, in such a fashion that both the rising **and**
the setting sun could be seen from any part **there-**
of. Also, the North Star and the Southern
Cross, each low in the heavens could be seen

by anyone standing upon the Plaza. The human
view was unobstructed from horizon to horizon,
so far as the power of the eye could penetrate.
This plaza was ample enough to hold in its confines every single member of the Atlantian nation
at one time. It was many acres in extent.
It is wonderful how many people can stand on
one acre, if they are only harmonious.

This great plaza was necessary for the Convocations, and the yearly ceremonies when all the
people went up to the Temple to receive guidance and instruction for the coming year. This
Convocation was always at the time of the Vernal Equinox when renewed impetus comes both
to the vegetable and the animal.

Thus the mountains partly cut down, left
space also for the facade which was tunneled into
for the interior of the building from the front,
and to this excavation additional structures were
added from time to time, to meet the necessities
of the Temple Colony. That is, wings were

built, and additional stories added, all with regard to the symmetry of the whole. The rooms
and colonnades all yielded to the unification of
the whole, which was the education of the Temple Staff, and through them of the whole people.

At the northeast corner, as I have already
mentioned, on the foundations of solid rock,
reaching far down into the earth, was builded
story after story a tower, upon this tower's top
was located the tallest observatory that has ever
been known in the world. There, they who
were wise, and who were considered best, after
having passed triumphantly through the intrica-
cies, the education and unfolding of the lower degrees, kept constant ward and watch. Out of
this tower, at its lower part, proceeded forth
over the great area, the wall of the Temple in-
closing the Great Hall of Convocation, and the
Temple proper, and from the Holy of Holies at
the bottom of the tower, Light, Strength and
Force, at times of Convocation, streamed forth

as the result of the united power of the Three, Five, Seven, Fifteen and Forty-five. But let us turn to a fuller description of the tower.

"The tower was 22½ feet in diameter at the highest point of the coping. It was built of hewn stone in the shape of the trunk of a tree, large at its base, growing a little smaller in diameter, half way up, and then widening again.

"This model from nature, was considered the strongest form. The stones, as I have said, were nicely cut and laid in a peculiar cement, found in the southern part of the Continent, which once hardened was as firm as the rock itself. So the tower bore itself aloft, as if it were one solid stone.

Over the top, at the distance of ten feet from the floor at the coping was a spherical dome. It was of glass, and more than that, it was made of a single piece, as transparent as water itself. Through this all the motions of the heavenly bodies could be seen and minuted from convenient points of observation, in the chamber below. The floor of the hall was of mosaic, wrought in figures, and when it shall reappear, he **who** is wise may read in this a history of the founding of the temple, its date, its object **and** the purposes to which it was dedicated.

At one edge there was set in the wall a circular disc that was movable at the time of the entrance or departure, for him who knew the secret spring. This was known only to the Three, **one** of whom was constantly on duty, in attendance on the "holy of holies," of this Temple. There was another "holy of holies" in the great Hall of Convocation, but that was the symbol of the highest person of the "Superior Wisdom." One was the Superior Wisdom and the other the Inferior Wisdom. Over this floor so tasselated was spread to protect it from injury, a carpet of heavy linen, woven so closely that it was almost impervious to impressions from without upon it. The usual wear and tear of things earthly, did

not affect it in the least.   This was stretched
tightly upon the whole floor. *U*pon the upper
surface of this was drawn a circle of the whole
circumference of the chamber. Within this per-
iphery were drawn three other circles,   which
joined each other at their circumferences, and
whose centers were each equally distant from the
center of the great circle.   Through these were
drawn the intersecting equilateral triangles and
the six-pointed star.   In the center of these inscribed circles was placed a seat, one for each
of the Three.   In the center of the great circle
was a tripod holding a censor, in which burned
the Eternal Fire.   In their invocations, when
they were reaching out to conquer new territory
in the invisible, it was absolutely necessary that
the potency of the Three should be embodied in
the outer circle.   Co-ordinate with this effort,
the potency of each must guard his own particular circle, while from the center it was essential should be wafted into space, the potency

which could call and conquer. These were all used upon especial occasions. These vigils were nightly and daily and the record of their observations were carefully kept. These three were wise men, for they had risen step by step from the knowledge of earthly things and their environments to a point where they could perceive all that could or would happen, not only to Atlantis, but to all the remainder of this planet.

They had also attained the point where other furnishings were not necessary for their assistance, for in the perception of the Divine Birthright, they declared themselves one with the All Potency, and so acted, so demanded and so perceived. This perception finally engendered pride of station, which conjoined to their knowledge, was the cause of their overthrow.

CHAPTER XIV

IN considering the remaining secret Chambers let us remember that all knowledge comes from the home of the Great Gods—the silence where everything is, that is.

Between the station of the Three and the Five, was a heavy floor of masonry, each stone of which fitted into all the others, even as one piece of solid rock is fitted into its surrounding rock. Had it all been one piece it could not have been more lasting nor more compact. The arch of the lower chamber was like the arch of the upper chamber. From the highest concavity of the lower ceiling to the floor of the upper chamber was three and eight-tenths feet of solid masonry. The arch of the lower chamber rested upon or sprang from five pillars in the walls of the circular chamber. Between each of these a single piece of marble was set, polished to the highest possible point. One was white, one was black, one was white, one was black and one was white. Between the two white ones was a band of burnished gold, the art of preparing which, after being lost for ages, was recovered again in Etruria, whose wondrous masterpieces are the marvel and glory of the present time. It glittered and shone, as only that metal can respond to the artizan's hand. These marble mirrors were turned towards the earth, at a slight angle, and in them could be seen, as in the pages of an open book, all things that were happening, had happened or were about to happen. That is to say, by the art of the Wise Ones, these had become reflectors of the Astral Books. Whoever knew the cipher could read, but to know the cipher they must be able to perceive, and no person could be eligible to membership in the Five, who under training did not manifest this power of perception. When the love of learning and the desire for understanding had given him the first rudiments of the cipher, he was transferred hither. Then, as if in a vision, he was allowed to give proof whether he could see and read. If he failed he was returned whence he came for further training, if it appeared the gift was his. If not, then only that which had happened to him was his as if he had dreamed it.

It is not necessary for me to say that the Five were rapid and accurate readers of whatever their wills sought to know. That which was good was perceived in the white mirrors. That which was evil or obstructive was seen in the black mirrors. So long as Atlantis was in its greatest power and glory, so long was the number maintained as I have described it. But during the last twenty-five years of the existence of the Temple in the city, the odd mirror in the white had clouded over in a singular fashion, growing darker and darker, until the final destruction, and to-day, under the waters there are three black and two white mirrors; but when the hour of redemption shall have struck, the stain will be wiped away from the white. Once more there will be three white and two black mirrors. In the records of the past, written on the floor of the upper chamber, there was this prophecy: "When the three are all black, swift destruction cometh to the Temple and the people."

This had been well known by those whose ambition should have led to higher and better things, and although they wondered at the continuous change for the worse, so clouded had their minds become by their selfish ambitions that no notice was taken of the dreadful warning.

Although the chamber was solid and there were neither windows nor doors, there were means of ventilation by which fresh air was conveyed into and out of this apparent tomb. The means of entrance were the same as those of the

upper chamber. Although no aperture communicated with the sunlight, yet apparently the light
from the great dome overhead, passed through
the solid masonry, as though it were glass. Whatever could be seen by the light in the upper
chamber, with its magnificent dome of crystal,
could just as easily be seen in the chamber of the
Five. On the floor of this chamber also was an
extremely fine, mosaic record of the nation, and of
the occult happenings to the same. Over this
was a carpet of the same material as that above,
and a circle twenty-two and eight-tenths feet in
diameter. Within this was drawn a pentagon,
thirteen and eight-tenths feet on a side. From
the center of each side of the pentagon to the
point of contact with the circle, a semi-circle was
drawn. In the center of the circle was a smaller
circle touching all the semi-circles, four and
eight-tenths feet in diameter. Where these semi-
circles intersected each other were four figures
resembling elipses. At the point corresponding

to the focus—the point farthest from the center, was the station of him who officiated. You will see when you draw these lines how intimately was the sustaining power of each bounded by the great circle of the environment. All were limited, supported and sustained. In the inner, the smaller circle representing with the center, the power of the One was reached and held by the semi-circle of each, and each was supported in turn by that of his brother, next to him, on the left, and by his own power, until the whole circle was completed.

Here the triangle has become the pentagon and the symbol of the intimate relations of those who are brothers was carried out fully and completely. All the civilization the world boasts to-day is the result of the vibrations set in motion within this noted tower of the Atlantians.

Between the divisions of the Three and the Five were three feet of solid masonry. The roof was arched as the heavens seem to be arched, and this arch was lined with an alloy of silver, gold and copper, an alloy which the citizens of the world to-day would give much to be able to imitate.

It was polished to the highest degree of finish, but strange to say, it did not reflect a single thing taking place in the chamber. It was supported in its place by seven pilasters: One of orichalcum, one of gold, one of silver, one of lead, one of tin, one of copper and one of platinum.

This was used instead of quicksilver, because the quicksilver could not be retained in place nor form, and the platinum was its opposite. On the plate of platinum at its base, was engraved the proportions of the alloy used in this great concavity.

There were always sounds emanating from it. Sometimes they were sweet **and** harmonious, sometimes sonorous and turbulent; for it did not reflect anything within **the** chamber. It was a reflector of the nation's sounds, and of all those

with whom they had dealings. It was in touch
with all the planets, and it was a curious fact
that in reflecting the sounds it also reflected the
colors of the sounds, because the same vibrations
that make sound produce color also. So you see
that in one chamber attention was called to the
working of the One in the Heavens, and in the
next chamber could be perceived the operations
of man's thought on the Astral plane, and in the
chamber of the Seven, we are now about to describe, the study was of the manifesting of thought
in its first potency. Thus in each grade, approaching nearer and nearer to those to whom
they ministered, and who should have been their
first care always, and above everything else their
supreme concern.

This chamber also, like the others, was permeated by the light which knows and recognizes
no obstruction. The light was of equal volume,
quality and quantity as that which lighted the uppermost chamber, and it had the same peculiarity

of penetrating and giving distinct view. It pervaded the whole chamber, without having any visible source. Upon this floor also was written in mosaic, as in the other chambers, a continuance of the history and progress of the nation and the city.

Over this, too, was spread, as in the other chambers, the carpet. Upon this carpet was a circle of twenty-one feet in diameter. Within this circle was described a heptagon, to the center were drawn radii, thus making each side of the heptagon the base of a triangle of which the two radii were the other two sides. Within each of these triangles was inscribed a circle, touching each of the sides. The center of these circles was the station of one of the Seven. In operating they might look to the center or the circumference, or to each alternately. But whatever was done was always with the utmost harmony and unity of potency.

There is still one more chamber of potent ef-

fort, that is the Chamber of the fifteen. The
Chamber of the forty-five was more that of a
school of training than a laboratory of occult
force. The thickness of the separating masonry
was seven feet. In the center it presented a square
rising above the roof of the Temple. Within it
was a square room with the sides facing each of
the points of the compass. Circular windows,
one each, pierced the walls of the four sides. The
one on the east was red, the one on the west was
blue, the south was yellow, and the north, white.

The floor was laid in tiles, and the tiles were
of a material which generations of wear could
not destroy. And upon these was a lesson which
contained absolutely, from beginning to end, all
the knowledge that man would ever need or could
expect to attain upon the earth. The wisest
might read it partially. To those lacking understanding, if they could decipher, it was still a
mystery and foolishness.

This may seem impossible, but it is true nevertheless, when man learns that all rays come from the One, it will not be such a difficult task to find the way to the source and origin of all that mystifies and perplexes him on the earth. It is because he believes there are many, and that the shadows and changing illusions are of the essence and quality of the real, that he diffuses his power and baffles his own inquiries.

In this Chamber, in a semi-elipse were fifteen seats, seven on each side of the keystone of the arch. The roof was also square. In one of the foci was a crystal globe, from which light always emanated. In the hours of rest it was necessary. In the hours of day, light from the outer permeated the room. The crystal globe hung midway from floor to ceiling without visible support, swaying gently with the movements of the thought currents about it. In the other focus of this semi-elipse three brazen serpents, supported on their tails and rearing upwards, held aloft in their mouths a censer in which burned the perpetual fire.

During the time of sessions, incense and perfumes fed by invisible hands, brought peculiar effects to those waiting for instruction and guidance. It was here, those who were fitted, after training in the school of the forty-five and waiting, were selected for admisssion under obligation for further training and practice. If they kept their obligation they then might sometime hope for promotion.

If they did not keep their obligation then they fell back. There was always more or less change going on in this chamber of trial. From these Fifteen, culled from the whole nation, came the Seven, Five and Three. Nor were they allowed to know of the powers beyond them, except they occupied the chair of the Elder Brother, who was their appointed leader and guide.

They came and went amongst the people, and were considered as persons of authority amongst the Temple Dwellers. They were but little removed from the forces lying below them, which they utterly and entirely controlled for the purpose of massing and using them for concentrated power.

This chamber rested upon the massive walls of the Forty-five by a ponderous arch, whose spherical edges met the solid rock, the buttressed foundation of the world, seemingly uplifted for the very purpose of this support.

Beneath the floor of the chamber of the Forty-five was hewn out the "Holy of Holies" of the Great Hall of Convocation, so that the mysteries intended and desired to be communicated, could be made manifest to the people at the stated times and seasons. This was the ultimate outcome of all this interlinking of organization.

The chamber of the Forty-five was twenty-five by twenty-five feet, and the walls were twelve feet thick. Within this wall, impervious to sound or impression from without, the students of this degree met. The chamber was so arranged, with its lofty, arched roof and solid floor of finest woods brought from all quarters of the earth, that the conditions of pure air were fully met. They who were sitting, sometimes for a shorter time, sometimes for days that seemed but hours, listened enchantedly to that which **was** propounded to them. There was no lack of understanding from crudeness or from any disarrangement of the physical conditions of harmony **and** peace, which all men must have, to be at the highest point of **perception.**

CHAPTER XV

THUS sitting, the Forty-five were arranged in four rows of seats, eleven in each row, arranged eliptically, facing a raised dais, on which sat the Elder Brother, during the hours of instruction. The rows of seats were raised one behind the other, and thus gave perfect and unobstructed liberty of sight and perception to the Brothers who sat upon them in the order of their ages. There was always close to the seat of the Elder Brother, another seat, and this, empty always to personal sense; to those who could see on the psychic plane was filled by an Elder Brother from the Invisible, as a mentor and guide, as an influencer of the Elder Brother of the visible, to receive whatever might be given either from his own knowledge, or by his coming in touch more readily with the invisible; thus receiving out of the realms of the Invisible that which was needed for instruction on any and all of the mortal-touched planes.

A narrow staircase was arranged in the thick wall, which led to the chamber of the Forty-five, and a sliding door, opening to the lightest touch of those who knew, admitted into the chamber. This chamber was ceiled and floored—sides, top and bottom, with wood they obtained from the country, to be known in the later days as South America, but then a large island. It was of a peculiar hardness, dark red in color, and susceptible of the most brilliant and lasting polish. It was so well fitted together that it seemed like one piece. They who were the builders controlled the elemental force, which was able to do persistently and in the finest manner, whatever it was set to do. So when the door was closed, it appeared as if they were in a shell from which there was no possible escape. There was no danger from any outer accident, except possibly an earthquake. But for many hundred years no earthquake had occurred. For many years to come none was predicted by even the wisest astrologers of the Temple. The doorway by which they entered was in the open end of the oval upon which the seats were placed. Within the whole chamber, at distances far enough to protect the sight of those who were receiving instruction, from any bewilderment by the light, points of emanating brilliancy were placed. What these points of light were composed of, hundreds of men in the days to come, will give several years of their lives to know, and never be able to find out.

Before these facts shall have again come into the possession of men, there will have been those who will have come to the place where their hands have laid, almost upon the thing they crave and so covet. These lights, held as it were by invisible torch-bearers, could be perfectly stationary for any length of time, or they could be moved as there was necessity for concentrating or diffusing that which they gave forth.

At times, in full view of the whole number, would come up something acting as a reflector of thought action and picturing either the Past or the Future. This great transparent blackboard, so to speak, so you may understand just what I am trying to say, held itself in place, or seemed to dissolve under the will of those who were instructing, and while one could see through it, it was an impermeable barrier to any passage through it; no thick bar of brass could more stoutly resist. While there was nothing of it that appealed to the sense of sight, there was still such force that it served as an obstruction, although invisible. Upon this clear sheet, of size large enough to fill the whole twenty-five feet, rising up as might be necessary, for the accommodation of whatever was thrown upon it, out of the mental conditions of those who taught under the law set up by those who in the highest

Chamber of the Temple, watched and waited through the Centuries. So in the times of instruction, the Elder Brother detailed whatsoever should come to him out of his own mentality, or should be given him out of the records of the Past, or out of that which should be the result of sequence, in the Future. At the same time he demonstrated upon this invisible screen, exactly as he described, both as to what had already occurred, or might take place. Did he desire to unfold a line of sequence, then as he talked of the sequence in a particular way, the whole company would see that all the sequences were alike; that everything moved forward on the line of the One Creative Thought, in perfect harmony for accomplishment of all events in manifestation. The things that seemed to happen were due to the perception of the investigator, and to the non-manifestation at the same time of the peculiarities appearing in the individual through which cognizance was made.

But let us describe one session: Minute by minute, there have been persons coming through the door into the chamber, which is held in the softness of a dim, pleasant twilight, not clear enough for perception, except at close range. They have quietly and without speaking, come forward each to the seats, where they have evidently been assigned, then, sitting, have restfully waited in silence and peace. In coming in, they have all advanced from the door of entrance across the space where the square of defonstration was held, thus showing as they came in, there was nothing between them and their seats.

They have passed on, and all are now seated. There was not a single absentee. Such a thing as absenteeism or tardiness in the workings of the Great Temple was unknown. Too well they knew the wonderful power of CONTINUOUS, UNBROKEN ACTION. The hour strikes from a sonorously-toned bell, semingly in the center of the room. To the personal sense, no bell is visible.

It might seem strange that we Atlantians had any idea of measuring time, but it must be remembered there is nothing not known; nothing that will ever be known; nothing that the world will ever receive, that was not received by those, who, eager for knowledge, were not only eager to understand, but to use. We had perceived and received all human knowledge.

As the hour strikes in the manner I have described, the forty-four and the Elder Brother looking up, perceived a form dim and misty in outline, has filled the chair of the presiding instructor. Sitting in the position of meditation, which in the later times the Egyptians copied in their Temple work, and left us on record, on their books of stone, they concentrate on the thought of unity.

There were three points upon which they concentrated in succession: *U*nity, Harmony and Love, for these three constitute the Unmanifested, so they who were in the Forty-five were

taught. When the quickening of the Invisible
within themselves had become exalted, at a sign
from the Elder Brother, they stood, and making
a sign that is recognized by both the visible and
the invisible, repeated words having of themselves potency, force and intense harmonious vibration. These words were reinforced by other
vibrations resembling the rolling sound of a great
organ. It was a reverberation partly reflected
and partly responsive, out of the Invisible by
which they received answer, and thus became
unified into the sense and condition of desire,
in its most perfect form for whatever might and
could be given· them. On this night of which
I am speaking, the Elder Brother commenced
describing the possibilities of unfolding in all who
were present; of the unfolding of the Earth's
condition; of the things that would bear down
in the way of clouds and darkness; of limitation,
obstruction and opposition, and as he described,
step by step, that which might come under cer-

tain circumstances, the screen of almost invisible material quivered and shimmmered with the lights and shades passing over it. To those who perceived with only the physical eye, there was only a dancing of lurid fires. To each who had come into more perfect condition, it was possible to perceive, not only the play of the light, but the varying colors and forms which lay behind the colors, not only upon the pictures of the scenes, but upon the scenes themselves. The Future presented itself as the Eternal Now. One of the Forty-five, looking forward, not dreaming that all that seemed to occur, was about to come in the close Future, hardly attempting to estimate time, saw then, how the Brotherhood of Wisdom, for the Ages, might find itself for a time unrepresented upon the earth; but, under the obligations which make the members of the Brotherhood acting, living members, whether living or dead, so the membership in the invisible sought, desired and brought about the remanifestation and rehabilitation. All the signs and points made and desired to be emphasized, were illustrated upon our screen. And thus, as the time went on, in that which was to be the dawn of a new recreation, so to speak, we perceived certain gatherings of the far Future were also being pictured upon the scren. I remember it all well, for it seemed, as the memory comes to me out of the Past, there was some responding condition within myself, not only did I see it and feel it, as regarding myself, but that others would then come into it at that time, whose presence and help would recall the now, but to be known then as ancient days, and they would testify to the truth of the then pictured.

I cannot tell you fully of all the drapings and decorations and precious metals that adorned this chamber, but you may imagine for yourselves nothing was spared to make it a fit place, both in the conditions of the visible and in the potencies of the invisible, drawn from all over the

world for the inculcating in its fullest and its
strongest, the truth of that which will be fully
verified. They who now in life, know not only
of the lower, but also of the higher, thus perceive the apparently futile in many respects has
for its governing, impelling force, the strength
and power of the ages behind it. All move on
to fulfill in the completed outline, whatever was
set and designed to be accomplished.

Thus the lessons given to the Forty-five were
either in voiced vibration, through the sense of
sight, or by thought transference. Whichever
method was used, the vibrations made themselves
plainly visible to the sense to which they were
addressed. Their vividness depended upon the
intensity with which the thought was projected.
But at all times, during a sessison of the Forty-
five, there were shadows more or less distinct
in outline, playing over this wonderful spectrum.

When instructions were being received from
the Three the play of forms and colors were

something that has never been seen elsewhere in the whole world. The reflections then obtained have really so impinged upon the Great Astral Record that the works accomplished have become mighty influences upon the Globe. The record of what these denizens of the secret chambers of the Great Temple thought and did, is one day to become supremely dominant in the affairs of the world. As the cycle rises to completion, it will become more and more potent. He who is wise and able, has thus given some outline.

CHAPTER XVI.

I HAVE tried thus far to give you a description of the Great Temple of Atlantis and of the Tower that was one of the wonders of the world. That which was in sight was not by any means all; even as the tree, bearing fruit after its kind above the earth, is by no means the largest nor most important part of the organic development. The organs of growth and transmutation are hidden from the curious eyes of the idle. So we have in the mid-heavens the angels and spirits of light; on earth mortals both visible and invisible; beneath the earth's surface are the beings belonging to the lower races, who have never been subjugated by the spiritual powers of such as held sway in the upper chambers.

These elemental beings will be classed in the later day as Salamanders, Water Spirits, Kobolds, Goblins and Dwarfs. They are workers in the Fire, the Water and the Earth or Rocks. It was in the internal fires of unregisterable heat, that during the latter days of Atlantis, the immense stores of gold and jewels, which the Temple Treasury held, were manufactured under PRIMAL CONDITIONS. In this also was illustrated the great law of Transmutation.

As the Great Tower flung itself toward the mid-heavens, pointing everlastingly upwards, it indicated the constant search man is making to the extent of his ability, for truth, light and potency. The part of the Tower that sank lower and lower into the bowels of the Earth, pypied the material and physical uses of that which was capable of transmutation. It also held within itself the lesson of the "Descent into Matter"— man's environments. So far as man himself was concerned, it held also the doctrine of the Three Brains. To all the world, both Atlantian and foreign the lesson was: "In the heavens above and the earth beneath, and the waters under the earth."

It has already been said that the whole city of Atlantis was arrayed in a splendor, whose glory was never equaled. Its buildings have never been surpassed, 'either in the symmetry of their architecture, in the material used, or in the tastefulness of its preparation and artistic designs. There was also a marvelous exhibition of gold and jewels, in a profusness carried up to the verge of the barbaric.

These means for personal adornment, were also used by all the people, even those in the humble walks of life, if Atlantis could be said to have had any such, the relations of poverty and riches long since had ceased to press on the attention of the nation. It was evident in the latter days that some source of almost limitless supply must be easily accessible. The Tower which lifted proudly its head on high, went down into the mountains the same distance, and the cellars and sub-cellars were occupied by beings who belonged to the lower races, who had been subjugated by the spiritual powers of those who held sway in the upper chambers.

None of the uninitiated knew for a certainty of that which was going on within the mountain. Only to the Three was this knowledge fully confided by the Builders. To them, long ago all material things which are deemed of any value by mortals, or of any use or importance whatever, had ceased to be of consequence, only so far as they might adorn or make beautiful, either the Temple or the City.

Underneath the Sanctuary, entered by a door opening into the solid rock, at the rear, was a flight of stairs leading down into a chamber hewn out of the rock. Out of this another staircase led into a similar chamber, and still another, and another, and yet another staircase and chamber.

Within these chambers were curious implements, fashioned for use in the operations of the workers. These operations required the use of certain materials, to make the manifesting and finishing of their work more easy. Their projected spirit power brought back the results produced by the various combinations. Many of these implements and operations will come into the hands of the re-incarnated Atlantians, from time to time, and more of them will not be given out except into the hands of the most trusted few.

In the First Cellar, Spirits of the Air labored and toiled, doing the will of the Masters.

In the Second Cellar, the Spirits of the Earth moved to and fro, intent on carrying out that to which they were set.

In the Third Cellar, Elementals whose forms but thinly clothed the fierce, blazing fires within, solved the varying problems of metallurgy.

In the Fourth Cellar, the lowest of all, the Spirits of the great, watery deep, fashioned whatever man needs and lays hold upon from their realm, either for use or adornment.

Vast tunnels led into the interior of the mountains and the Continent, from each of these cellars. The spirits of the air by a spiral course, ascended to the highest points of the mountains, and here communicated with their fellows in the outer world, receiving supplies.

The tunnel from the Cellar of the Earth Spirits opened into an inaccissible part of the mountain, on a little plateau, which was constantly guarded by an impenetrable veil of fog.

The tunnel of the Fire Spirits led under the Continent, diagonally down to the volcanic fires of the Earth.

The tunnel of the Water Spirits communicated directly with the seas by the shortest feasible route.

In the center of the mountain was a cave-like room, which was the Treasury of the Temple. This storehouse communicated with all four of the tunnels, and by a secret entrance, with the Temple itself. It was not only the Treasury of the Temple, but of the nation as well.

He who knew the secret of the Treasury would stand in the rear of the Moly Holy Place, at the hour of high noon, on a certain day of the year, and watch until by a peculiar arrangement of the polished marbles, a single ray of sunlight thrown from the chambers above would be reflected upon the wall at the back. This could only be seen when the observer was in a particular position, and then but for a period of three minutes. Having perceived this, he would turn one quarter to the right, and move seven steps in a straight line, then turning to his original position, he took five steps more, and then turning one-quarter to the left, three steps brought him to an apparently blank wall, highly ornamented. But to him who had the key, a slight pressure on a jewel of immense value, apparently placed there for ornamentation, opened a huge door of rock, weighing tons, but so balanced that it moved easily and without noise, and was screened from view by the shrine which stood in front. Entering boldly, as soon as he stepped upon the flagging inside the door, the great stone settled back into its first position. It could be opened on the inside by pressing upon a slight projection at the back. Thirteen times thirteen steps brought him again to a blank wall, through a high, arched passage, lighted by the never-dying lights produced by the action of positive and negative earths combined with the rock, which gave out an electrical phosphorescent light, the secret of which perished with the nation, but which may be recovered at a later day by the chemists, as those who are expert in safes, recover the forgotten combination of the locks thereof. Once more, he who knew the secret spring, might open and pass within. The Treasure Chamber opened to the Temple Inspector on the day of the Vernal Equinox, when the sun went down in the West.

CHAPTER XVII.

IT was a sight that met his gaze, which an avarice-tainted soul would never be allowed to contemplate. Great heaps of gold, silver and aluminum, the method used by us for obtaining which, was the result of condensed electrical power, acting through surcharged magnets of the finest steel. In the times to come the forces of induction will, for a time, be very little understood. But the day will come when they will have the very best method of extracting aluminum from the original clay as their secret. These stacked up heaps of the noble metals were in quantity sufficient to last for centuries, nor had their continuous production ceased, but every day added to the increasing store.

Beside these, were heaps upon heaps of price-

less jewels, some of them still warm from the
fires of earth and water, in which they were crys-
tallized. Both the polished and the uncut glittered and shone here in the light which was as
full and strong as in the passage-way.

Here the workers in the various cellars deposited the results of their labors. From here
the civil rulers received whatever they needed,
upon sudden pressure, in their traffic with all outside nations of the earth. But there were also
in the city their own storehouses and treasuries
of wealth. This was only that which belonged
to the Temple, and was the result of the labors
of the servants of the Temple. In case of necessity, the civil rulers could draw upon the Temple
for reserves in any amount.

No human eye hath seen, nor any tongue described the immensity of the wealth lying to this
day, in that strong, mountain treasury beneath
the waves. There is enough gold lying in it to
destroy the value of the gold now in use upon

the earth. But when the day of its discovery shall come it will belong to a nation, who shall have so purified itself from avarice that there shall be no karmic weight transferred from this treasure to the shoulders of its finders.

Upon the inner door that opens into this treasury rests a seal. Upon this seal is the following inscription: "The potent Will of the Most Mighty holds this treasure safely, until the time of the restoration shall come. The Angel of the waters has charge of it."

It seems hardly necessary to say that the jewels and gold were all manufactured by the occupants of the cellars, and that it was the reflection out of the Astral light, on the vision of the clear-sighted, that made so many earnest believers in the transmutation of base metals into gold and jewels.

CHAPTER XVIII.

THE manner of adjustment and Convocation was after the following fashion: As has already been stated, the priesthood had charge of the education of the people. There were some better fitted for one thing than another, as even at the present day. But those who were especially gifted with understanding, who combined reverence with intense desire for the knowledge of that which was unseen and hidden, wherever found, were transferred to the temple service, and this was the first step in the separation of the wheat from the chaff.

Those, who in their training, as part of the Temple family, exhibited a still higher degree of intelligence and perception were again set aside for the Forty-five, and again in the same manner for the Fifteen. The selection for the higher

Chambers followed in the same order, from those best developed and adapted to the work to be done. The training of the Forty-five was first, submission to unseen guidance, in a more intense degree than as ordinary scholars of the Temple. When they had reached the point where, because they were asked, they took pains to think out along any line that ought or might be desired, their power for broad, intense contemplation had increased until their meditations had become second nature.

The next step was concentration. Notice the steps, submission, meditation, concentration. When the thought was well massed and the vibrations were uniform and persistent, then they were taught to project the concentered thought which had been the essence of their meditations. As the absolute *Unity*, IT meditates, as the Divine Ideation, It concentrates, as the Creative Thought, It projects. So nearly as the Earth-dweller may follow this line of procedure, so nearly will he be able to lay hold of the *U*nseen force and make it available for all good purposes.

Years of discipline in the Forty-five and still later in the Fifteen, made each member of the Seven ready and expert in these labors. The perfection was carried still farther in the Five, where they practiced the attracting of the vibrations of unseen force, of any kind whatever into alignment with their own projection, thus controlling the powers of the great names.

It was as if workmen taking a ball **of** soft metal from the crucible or furnace, should whirl it rapidly in the air, until it had assumed a certain form, and then launch it forth to fulfill their will.

But to the Three, belonged **the** directing of **all** the force thus gathered. **Nor** was there allowed to be any chance for mistake, not even a clashing thought in the minds of the Three. It **was** always determined by the casting **of lots, who** should control the outward moving of the vibrations at any Convocation, and to the power of the one of the Three, the other two added their potency. The regular Convocations were under the Full Moon of each month. But the special Convocations were under the will of the Three. When special Convocation was desired, the word given at the last Convocation WAS whispered to each, out of the Invisible, in such a manner, that all could recognize and understand the call.

At the close of the Convocation, the Elder Brother of each Section received from the Elder Brother of the highest Section, a word like this: "Myld." This the Elder Brother communicated to the inner sense of the instructed (it never being spoken aloud), as the closing password of the session.

If there was a special Convocation, then, to each one, came out of the Silence, the Word to the inner ear, and thereby not only was the day named, but the hour was fixed, being always at a certain distance from the Sun's setting. If there was no special Convocation, then at the nxt regular meeting, each one present at the opening, in succession, in low breath, pronounced the given word, so that which had been given out, was again recalled.

The work was formally opened in the upper Chamber by the Three. At the first word of invocation, the "Center of Fire" glowed and flashed, and whatever had been planned or arranged for, needing potency was apportioned amongst the lower chambers. In the chamber of the Five, the polished marble slabs reflected the orders. In the chamber of the Seven, the notes of the bell, like the tones of some sweet harmony, told the story. But to the trained inner ear of the Elder Brother, in the Fifteen, as by inspiration, came that which was necessary to be done.

There was no hesitation in compliance, no timidity in obedience, and no delay in action.

The gathered force of the whole nation, in charge of the Forty-five were sent forward to the **Fifteen**, and there, as intensified was passed on to the Seven, where, bound together, solidified and shaped, the projected potency was again handed on to the Five, who harmonized the activity of the potent vibrations with the vibrations of the Universe. Thus changed, from the Special to the Universal, it was placed in the hands of the Three, who uniting their force in the **One**, stood ready to hurl into space, in all the awfulness of power, this projection of the concentrated **potency** of a nation, by which they could really expect to hold and keep everything **they** had seized upon.

The matter of training cannot be understood from mere description. Only when students attempt of themselves to bring their mental conditions under subjugation, can be understood, how long it takes to accomplish **the** wonderful things done by our Ancient Brothers.

CHAPTER XIX.

THEY who ruled in Atlantis, as the priest-hood, were successful in guiding the ship of State wisely and fortunately, so long as they considered the interests of the whole nation as one. As long as they put aside the sense of separateness, while they only sought for wisdom, that the benfit growing out of it might be utilized in common by all the nation, who looked for light and guidance from them, all was well. As long as the Three, Five and Seven, with the Fifteen and Forty-five were separate and yet one, the only distinction being, to see who could best work with the highest potency in the position where he was placed, satisfied that the well and perfect doing and the acquiring of knowledge from experience, would bring the reward that comes always to attainment.

They looked to the perfect doing, and not to the result, and out of this desire grew the concentration of potency in their hands, which made them the one nation of the earth exceeding all others in the unravelling of the hidden mysteries. But it was not a task of idle floating, but sometimes of fierce, desperate warfare in the domains of the Invisible. As one point after another unfolded to their perceptions, those who held guard over the hidden truths, or those who wrought ignorantly or malevolently to confuse mortal understanding, used every effort to upset, and if it were possible, to cut off the keys of the Universal principles. And it was many years, aye centuries, before they had compassed the fact that numbers harmoniously united and agreed upon a certain, single point, on spiritual lines, were just as powerful as the combinations on the physical plane, with the difference that if spiritual conditions were once perfectly trained and harmónized, there could be no defection nor sudden weakness, for weakness is in no sense a spiritual attribute. While an army, or other mass of physical conditions might at any time be stampeded.

Therefore, in all the work, none were admitted to the separate and secret assemblies until the overcoming of the body and its desires was far advanced, thus leaving the Spirit a clear field in which to operate.

Another point, so soon as the occult ideas and thoughts were strongly developed, it served as a magnet for those who were in or on the same lines of thought, both from the incarnating spheres, and also from other points upon the earth, where lamps lighted from the Atlantian torch, by its inspiring reflection, had stimulated those who came within its reach, to a higher and more vigorous search. Knowing of Atlantis, they gravitated thither, and here they would have remained and shared with Atlantis the fate that overtook her, blotting out for a time from the earth, all the knowledge that went before, had not those, who in the Silence of the *U*nseen, watched and foreseen the cataclysm (but not its cause), worked to scatter abroad upon the earth, enough to become the seed and salt of salvation for the generations that have followed.

In all the movements of the earlier day, the segregation and massing unavoidably led to the pressing forward to the front, upon the development, along the new lines, of some one who could become, under inspiration, a leader. This was all well, excpt as the world always resents and resists the aggressiveness of new ideas, with the knife, the fagot, the scaffold, and in later days with the subtiler force of mind, thus crushing, torturing and destroying the instruments or leaders.

They who were the depositaries of knowledge for the time being, thus suffered ignominious death. The knowledge itself has been in great danger from the machinations of secret enemies, of total eradication from the earth and the **per-**ceptions of its inhabitants. This was likely to happen before its firm establishment could be accomplished. This fact was well known and understood by the malign forces. Upon this knowledge they acted, again and again, seeking to have the leaders in occult movements either bring destruction upon themselves or have others entirely cut them off.

Therefore, those having this matter in charge, have resolved instead of teaching men through the tongue and brain of a Brahma, or a Jesus, His place should be supplied by a sodality of many welded into one. But even her they stand face to face with another obstacle. It has been an essential, that if the truth be preserved, individuality must increase in its perception and reality, and in the latter days they will be confronted with the intense individuality of the people, who are confused and overcome by the sense of separateness. They who seek to study on these lines, and to gain wisdom, must as it were, train the units, made up of members, into a oneness or individuality of the whole and thus shall be born a new MESSIAH, or a new Truth. The Christos of that Great Cycle, will be a union of many individuals, or a nation who shall stand as the representatives of the new unfoldment of Truth.

In the Record of the Adepts, there is a vision described as seen by one of the Mighty Ones; of an image whose head, body and limbs were made up of different metals, and the feet were of iron and aluminum. Each of these metals represented a Messianic age, a new Truth, and an Empire directly relatinfg to some manifestation of that truth. These will represent the leaders of the previous dispensations, and then follows the vision, a stone cut out of the mountain without hands, which represents a nation fashioning itself, until it shall have obtained MESSIAHSHIP, and thus more powerful, it shall overshadow in its manifestation and dispensation all that has come before. ALL who are looking toward the light, ALL who are seeking unselfishly for wisdom, must, as constituent parts of that nation, attain such light, such wisdom; and drawing closer and closer together, like drops of mercury when they touch, they shall become as one. For this we work and wait.

CHAPTER XX.

A MONG the archives of that time and country has come to the knowledge of our present generation, the following prophecy:

"And it shall come to pass in those days, in which the highest knowledge that has ever been given to the world, shall be seized upon by the few, and if rightfully and truthfully held for the many, will bring to all those who shall come upon the earth, wisdom, blessing and growth. But there must also be an overcoming of the natural and physical, which will bring disturbance and sore distress, because the physical yields not to the rule of the Spirit, without much resistance. All progress in the soul's career is stimulated by the instinct of the Spirit to return to the condition of its first powers and estate, before it

should have individualized itself from the ONE.
It is no sin, nor crime to seek to know, by all
the means within the power of the Spirit to grasp
or undertake. Nor does the ONE resent as sin,
such attempts. On the contrary, IT intends that
they who have become individualized, shall sooner
or later, enter into all knowledge. That is the
perfect attainment. It shall come to pass, whoever fits the self for knowledge, shall receive it,
but whoever attempts to grasp potency without
being fitted to handle it, serious consequences will
ensue, and the thing already attained, may be
taken away. There can be no sin for those who
shall have knowledge, in the grasping of the very
highest in their pursuit; but if they shall seek,
before they have made themselves ready to grasp
that which is withheld, simply by their own force
of potency, disregarding the consenting, or the
law of the ONE, then there will come dire results, or if it so happen that the nation shall have
so far advanced that their knowledge would be

dangerous to the other nations of the world, in its use, then will it be withdrawn. But this is true, that the physical man is of no value, only as an agent in the computation of the happenings upon the earth. While it might seem to man an awful thing that millions of bodies should cease to exist, there was nothing in that issue that could be charged against the leaders. That was something distinct, by itself, and something that fulfilled the law. The thing for which the leaders suffered was disobedience of the law, which denied to the created the forceful taking from the ONE, any knowledge, for which the taker is not prepared.

When limited power meets *U*niversal potency, there can't be but one issue. So now under stand, there was no sin, but simply the outcome of the law of the *U*niverse. Even the intense desire, which might seem a sin, was in one sense lawful, and the result of causes implanted by the Creative Thought itself. They were not responsible, but they were the instruments. It was necessary that the law should be proved. It has always been a saying of the Wise Ones, that those things which seem to be great disasters to the earth-dwellers, must come to pass, and instruments must be used for that purpose. But these instruments standing in the front, must suffer for that which they have provoked.

As to the outlook for accomplishment. The instruments of the mighty forces of the *U*nseen evidently have not developed the strength we desire, nor that is necessary, for the perfect culmination. Until further training can develope proper concentration, they seek to bridge over and to hold as much as possible of that which has already been gained.

CHAPTER XXI.

By way of addenda, and to show that this book has authoritative substance for its assertions and information, we give our readers a couple of clippings from the mass of newspaper flotsam and jetsam, of the last years.

The following is the *Maya* account of the destruction of Atlantis, from Dr. Augustus Le Plongeon's rendering of the Troano manuscript:

"The year six *Kan,* on the eleventh *Muluc,* in the month *Zac,* there occurred terrible earthquakes, which continued without intermission until the thirteenth *Chuen.* The country of the hills of mud, the 'land of *Mu,*' was sacrificed. Being twice upheaved, it suddenly disappeared during the night, the basin being continually shaken by volcanic forces. Being confined, these caused the land to sink and rise several **times** and in various places. At last, the surface gave way, and the ten countries were torn asunder **and** scattered into fragments; unable to withstand the force of the seismic convulsions, they sank with sixty-four millions of inhabitants, eight thousand years before the writing of this book."

The other extract is of one of the buildings which reincarnated Atlantians put up, when they held sway in the land of the Nile, centuries after the destruction of their own beloved country:

"Some months ago, while workmen were engaged in an attempt to restore the partly fallen Hypnostyle Hall of the great Temple of Karnac, in Egypt, eleven columns gave way and fell. This was some months ago. Thirteen columns had fallen in ancient times, and it was while preparations for their restoration were being made, that the others fell, and three others were so shaken as to compel removal.

"Our archaeological readers will be delighted

to learn that hundreds of Arab laborers, under the direction of able engineers, are now engaged in restoring those ancient ruins, the largest and best preserved of any in Egypt which have reached these times.

"All of these twenty-seven columns will be reconstructed and placed in their original position. The uppermost member of each column weighs 1242 tons. The architraves weigh 25 tons each.

"Modern engineering processes are not equal to the task of reconstructing this work, so a huge inclined plane, requiring 100,000 cubic meters of earth, after the manner of the ancient architects, will be constructed and removed when the work is finished, which it is expected will be completed by May of 1904.

"In December last M. Legran, in charge of the work, came upon a wonderfully beautiful bust of one of Egypt's olden gods. Other portions of the statue have subsequently come to light, and it is hoped the residue may be found and restored to its entirety, save, possibly, a small piece to complete one of the legs. This statue, labeled 'Khonsu of Thebes, God of the Day, will be placed in the reconstructed Temple, and it is expected other treasures of ancient art will be unearthed in the farther removal of the debris of ages which has accumulated in these ruins."

FINIS